GENTLEMAN ROGUE

BARBARA NEIL

Harlequin Books

TORONTO • NEW YORK • LONDON
AMSTERDAM • PARIS • SYDNEY • HAMBURG
STOCKHOLM • ATHENS • TOKYO • MILAN
MADRID • WARSAW • BUDAPEST • AUCKLAND

Published August 1993

ISBN 0-373-31203-2

GENTLEMAN ROGUE

ONE: Shown the Door

THE FIRST GENTLEMEN of Nardingham, a hamlet in the north of England, were gathered in the chambers of Mr. Aycock, the lawyer, who leased two rooms above the greengrocer's in the market square. All eleven of the gentlemen stood save one, who, it would be accurate to say, lounged rather than sat. He was also the only one in the room who smiled.

Mr. Aycock approached the smiling gentleman, who had availed himself of his best and only chair and now made himself quite at home in it. "Mr. Starr," the lawyer ventured, "it has come to our attention that there have been some slight, um, irregularities in the manner in which you have conducted your, um, affairs since arriving at Nardingham."

"*Slight* irregularities?" Mr. Starr replied, as though offended. "I assure you, sir, the Starrs do nothing *slightly.* If there are irregularities, and I am certain you are too honourable a fellow to lie about such a thing, they may be *immense, appalling,* or *monstrous,* but never *slight.*"

Abashed, Mr. Aycock looked at the other gentlemen. One of them, a man, possessed two farms, six daughters and one wife, jabbed the lawyer with his elbow to prod him on. "Get to the ladies," he hissed in his ear.

Clearing his throat, Mr. Aycock proceeded, "If I may continue."

"By all means," said Mr. Starr with a gracious sweep of the hand. "You were speaking of the deplorable irregularities in the conduct of my affairs. Pray continue."

Clearing his throat, the lawyer asserted, "You call yourself Mr. Ryder Starr and claim to be nephew to the now deceased Lord Matchless and cousin to the present Lord Matchless."

"I do not *claim* to be Ryder Starr. I *am* Ryder Starr, and those *are* my illustrious relations, both past and present. My travelling companion, Mr. Nussle, can vouch for the truth of all I have said. Is that not correct, Nussle?"

The lofty personage thus referred to stood at the door wearing an expression that dripped disdain. Unlike Mr. Starr, he was no longer in the prime of manhood and he did not smile; nor, the townspeople conjectured, had he ever smiled in his life. Called upon to speak, Mr. Nussle declared, "That is correct."

"Exactly so," said Mr. Starr, thoroughly satisfied.

Mr. Aycock was not satisfied, however. "You gave us to understand," he said, "that you were a, um, gentleman."

On hearing this, Mr. Starr's smile became more engaging. "I received my education at Oxford. Consequently, I am a gentleman."

Once again the farmer poked Mr. Aycock and hissed, "Get to the ladies."

After a baleful look at his fellow townsmen, the lawyer summoned up his most imposing air and said, "We have reason to believe, sir, that, um, fraud has been, um, perpetrated."

Affecting shock, Mr. Starr replied, "I cannot and will not believe such a thing. I have never known the good people of Nardingham to be anything but honest and upright in their dealings with me. If you intend to accuse any of them of defrauding me, you had better have irrefutable proof of it, sir."

On this, the landholder with the six daughters pushed his way forward, bore down on Mr. Starr and growled, "It is you who've defrauded us and are no better than a thieving rascal. You've represented yourself as a philanderer, which is a fabrication and a lie."

"*Philanthropist,* you mean, Farmer Guggins. If I were a philanderer, it would be shockingly *outré* to admit it."

"Never mind what you call yourself. You've taken money from our womenfolk, claiming it were for charity, flirting with them and making up to them so as they'd hand over their shillings without giving any thought to what their husbands and brothers and fathers might have to say to it. If that ain't fraud, I'd like to know what the devil it is!"

Mr. Starr regarded the irate farmer with interest. "You wound me, sir," he said. "Indeed you do. You imply that only the ladies have supported my philanthropic efforts, when, in fact, each of you gentlemen has reached into his heart and purse on behalf of the Samaritan Hospital. Moreover, you imply that I have gained personally by my philanthropies."

"I imply nothing. I say so, straight out. You have pocketed the money yourself!"

Whipping out a scented handkerchief, Mr. Starr applied it to the corners of his lips, which gave a hint of quivering, whether with distress or laughter, it was difficult to say. "Do you all think as Farmer Guggins does?" he asked the others in the room. "Are you all convinced that I am no better than a charlatan?"

Having consulted one another with their eyes, the gentlemen, to a man, nodded their heads in a staunch affirmative.

"It pains me, my good friends, to be suspected, but when has true goodness ever been appreciated, at least in its own time?" He closed his eyes and shook his head.

Mr. Aycock cleared his throat and said, "We have brought you here today, Mr. Starr, to invite you to, um, return the money you have, um, accepted in the name of the hospital. If you do not, we shall be, um, obliged to inform the magistrate."

Mr. Ryder Starr opened his eyes. "Good friends, I am obliged to tell you I cannot return the money."

"Ha!" cried the farmer. "I knew it. He's gambled it away—or worse!"

Mr. Aycock leaned forward to inform Mr. Starr, "As you refuse to, um, return the money, I am afraid we shall be obliged to inform the magistrate. I fear you shall soon find yourself in, um, jail, sir."

"I cannot return the money, my esteemed friends, for the most excellent of reasons—to wit, I have, as promised, sent it to the Ladies' Association for the Samaritan Hospital. Haven't I, Nussle?"

Nussle inhaled and said, in the manner of one who was obliged to tolerate malodorous company, "You have. I posted the money myself."

"Exactly so," said Mr. Starr.

The gentlemen of Nardingham looked at one another in consternation.

Mr. Starr confounded them further by saying, "If you do not believe me, my friends, let me invite you to enquire of Benjamin Puissant, Esquire, of London. He lately received in the post the sum of seventeen pounds, to be donated to the Samaritan Hospital. Mr. Puissant will not know me by name, as I prefer to remain anonymous in my philanthropic dealings. However, he will know me by my private insignia, which I shall be pleased to divulge to Mr. Aycock in secret, should he desire to write Mr. Puissant, who is renowned for his integrity and is a lawyer with a rising reputation, like yourself, Mr. Aycock."

Following a moment of indecision, the gentlemen of the village gathered in a corner to confer. While he awaited their verdict, Mr. Starr returned his handkerchief to its place in his sleeve and waited patiently.

When the conference ended, Mr. Aycock announced, "We have concluded that you would not have offered the name of, um, Benjamin Puissant, Esquire, if he were not able to, um, corroborate your statement, either because you have indeed done as you claim and sent him the money or because you have bribed him to say so. We, therefore, um, withdraw all threat of arrest and instead require that you quit Nardingham before, um, nightfall."

As was his custom, Mr. Starr smiled. "That is not very hospitable of you," he observed pleasantly, "to invite a gentleman to leave your quaint little hamlet in the space of but two hours. I dare say the ladies may have some objections to offer."

A buzzing now filled the chamber as the gentlemen conferred once more. At last, Mr. Aycock stepped from the anxious huddle to say, "We must insist, sir, that the ladies not be, um, apprised of your imminent departure."

Mr. Starr rose from his chair. "Do you expect me to quit Nardingham without so much as saying farewell to those many gracious women who were so kind as to befriend me these past weeks, to support my poor charitable endeavours, and to open their homes and hearts to me?"

The farmer answered plainly, "If you dare to say boo to any of them, you're as dead as a pig in a peat bog."

Mr. Starr regarded the farmer. "Mr. Guggins, permit me to compliment you upon your powers of persuasion," he said with a bow. Turning to the others, he declared, "As you are all honourable gentlemen and as you would not comport yourselves so cruelly unless you truly believed I had somehow wronged you, I am prepared to quit Nardingham exactly as you request."

"You are?" Mr. Aycock said. The assembly squinted at each other in surprise at the ease with which they had won their point.

"Oh, yes. Nothing gives me greater joy than the prospect of obliging such good friends as yourselves. However, I must beg three small favours before I go."

With narrow eyes, the farmer demanded, "What favours?"

"Merely these—first, that you grant me a bit of assistance, as I find myself with pockets to let at present and am unable to take myself out of Nardingham without settling one or two debts. In addition, I require a bit of the ready in order to make the journey from Nardingham to a destination as yet unknown. Seventy-five pounds will do, I expect."

A gasp went round the room.

"It is little, I know, for a gentleman of my breeding, but I have renounced the life of luxury and ease and wish nothing more than to be able to continue my work for the Samaritan Hospital."

"Seventy-five pounds?" cried Mr. Aycock, who was reeling from the magnitude of the figure.

"And in addition to the funds, I request that you supply me with a letter of character, signed by all of you."

The farmer nearly choked.

"In this letter, you will recommend me to the acquaintance of other honourable gentlemen such as yourselves in other delightful villages such as Nardingham."

"Villages *far* from Nardingham, I trust," the farmer said darkly.

"As far from Nardingham as the stagecoach can carry me. You have my word on it, as a gentleman."

"Seventy-five pounds and a letter of character," Mr. Aycock mourned. "Heaven help us all."

"My third and most important request is this," Mr. Starr continued, "that under no circumstances will any of you reveal a word of these proceedings to my cousin, Lord Matchless." At the mention of this noble name, his voice grew reverent. It seemed to tremble as he spoke. "If my cousin should hear that I have sullied the family name in any way, however innocently, he should be deeply angry, I assure you, so angry that I cannot vouch for what he might do. Indeed, he might cut me entirely. That would be punishment indeed. Nothing is so painful as estrangement from those one loves and admires and is utterly dependent upon."

The gentlemen heard these last words with interest. Indeed, compared with the first two requests, this one came as a ray of sunshine comes to a cat drenched by rain. Mr. Starr had given them the means of avenging themselves upon him, and they would not fail to seize the opportunity.

Mr. Aycock invited him to step into the outer chamber with his servant while they conferred. Wishing the gentlemen good luck in their disputation, Mr. Starr strode from the room.

"SEVENTY-FIVE POUNDS!" Nussle groaned. "Permit me to observe, Master Ryder, we can never squeeze such a sum out of them. This time you have gone too far."

"Be easy," Mr. Starr said with a laugh. "We shall get it—or nearly so. It will be worth it to them to be rid of me. Their only concern will be scaring it up before the ladies get wind of my leaving."

"My word, the ladies! They will not like it. They will kick up a dreadful dust." Nussle sniffed, making it clear that he anticipated nothing but mischief from that quarter.

"The ladies will be desolate, it is true. My arrival provided them with entertainment such as they have not met with in many a year, perhaps in their entire lives."

Nussle raised his brow. "*Entertainment,* you call it!"

"Of the first water. Not only have they been granted the opportunity to flirt with a young gentleman, who, if I may say so, is well formed in both face and figure, well mannered, versed in all topics suitable to polite conversation, and, by their lights, fashionably dressed, but they have been able to do it all in the name of charity. What more could any female confined in the country and bored to extinction ask?"

"She could ask for marriage," Nussle offered, "and I expect she will, sir, if you do not have a care."

Mr. Starr considered. "You refer, no doubt, to Miss Guggins. I believe she does cherish some notion of tying me up in connubial knots. But we shall be gone from this place before she has another opportunity to accost me. And by the by, Nussle, you promised you would not call me 'sir.' It is some time since you were butler at Broome Court, you know."

"May I be so bold as to speak candidly, Master Ryder?"

"Certainly, Nussle. And, as I have repeatedly said, you need not address me as 'Master Ryder.' You are no longer a servant. You are my travelling companion."

"Thank you, Master Ryder, sir. I am sure I know how to comport myself properly in our situation, awkward though it be. I pride myself on knowing my place, even if you have a lamentable tendency to forget it."

Mr. Starr smiled. "I fear you are a snob, Nussle."

"Yes, sir, but as you are not, I trust you will forgive my overstepping myself when I observe that it was perhaps unwise to send the seventeen pounds to London. If the gentle men of Nardingham do not see fit to make you a present of the seventy-five, we shall have nothing to live on.''

"As I have explained before, good friend, we must be completely honourable in regard to the charity money, else we might one day find ourselves not merely threatened with arrest, but arrested in fact. As long as we can prove that the money has been sent to its proper destination, we shall keep ourselves free of leg shackles.''

"But why must it be the Samaritan Hospital? Surely there are benevolent associations that do not require one to repeat such unseemly tales of misery and squalor. Is there not a charity that is somewhat more refined, sir?''

"Oh, surely, my squeamish friend, I have told you why it must be the Samaritan Hospital and no other.''

"I believe you meant to, but our conversation was interrupted, by the appearance of a young lady. Far be it from me to condemn a gentleman's indulgence of the whims of the fair sex, sir, but they frequently interrupt our conversations, it seems.''

"Yes, and a more pleasant interruption I cannot imagine. But to return to the Samaritan Hospital, you deserve to know the full truth, Nussle. I recollect I was sitting in a tavern, glancing over the *Post*, and thinking what I might do to collect my inheritance. I was dreadfully discouraged, as you well know, for my cousin not only refused to receive me, but he ignored my letters. Suddenly, as I was wondering if there was a way of catching his attention, my eyes fell to the bottom of the page. There I saw a list of charity subscriptions, and I had the answer. I closed my eyes and pointed a finger. When I opened them, I had pointed to the Samaritan Hospital, refuge of unfortunate females. As Mr. Benjamin Puissant was listed as its agent, I sent to him for a pamphlet detailing the progress and proceedings of the charity.

Thanks to his prompt response, I was supplied with facts so heart-rending as to move even the hardest of hearts.

"The very next day, I set out for Clodham, to which you were so kind as to accompany me. The ladies of the village heard my pleas on behalf of the hospital with generous hearts and soon demonstrated their good will in pecuniary terms. Naturally, upon hearing of these donations, the gentlemen of the town began to suspect me. When I had given them sufficient hints of skulduggery, they were willing to pay me to leave their charming village without delay. You will recall that before we quit Clodham, you posted to Mr. Puissant the sum of six pounds. We have been sending him sums for the hospital ever since. I trust he is properly grateful."

"But not as grateful as the gentlemen who have bribed you to leave their villages. I confess, I did not think they would be so anxious to be rid of you as to pay such sums."

"It is true, I have become wonderfully proficient at making myself unwelcome. What is the calculation thus far?"

Nussle removed a small book from the pocket of his waistcoat. "From Clodham, twenty-three pounds sixpence. From Upchalk, thirty-one pounds, three shillings and ninepence. From Littledell, forty-two pounds, seven shillings, and threepence."

"Our profits multiply."

Putting the book away, Nussle said, "May I enquire, sir, what good are our profits if the gentlemen do not do as you wish in regard to your cousin?"

"You are too bleak, Nussle. Of course they will do as I wish."

"That is what you said the last time, if I may point out, sir, and the time before that, but naught has come of it thus far."

"Be of good cheer. We have every reason to hope. Did you observe how their eyes shone when I pleaded with them not to tattle on me to my cousin? All thoughts of their precious seventy-five pounds flew from their minds. Visions of retaliation quickened their heartbeats. I dare say we shall not be gone two minutes from this place before they will have written a letter to Lord Matchless informing him of my dastardly conduct."

"But will his lordship act on it? He has done nothing as yet. Perhaps we would do better to forget the entire matter."

Mr. Starr's insouciance disappeared. Across his handsome countenance flashed a look of anger. "I should never have the face to look at myself in the glass if I permitted myself to forget."

Nussle bowed his head. "I confess, I cannot forget it either, sir. Nor shall I forget that my late lord, breathing his very last, charged me with your care."

Shaking off his dark humour, Mr. Starr clapped the butler on the shoulder and declared, "And care for me you have, Nussle. I thank you with all my heart."

Lest Mr. Starr grow indecorously sentimental, Nussle turned the subject. "The question remains, will Lord Matchless come round this time?"

"I do not know what my cousin is like to do. All I know is that we are bound to force his hand soon. He cannot withstand these assaults on the family name very much longer."

On that, the door opened and Mr. Aycock gestured to them to return to his inner chamber.

Mr. Starr took one look at the lawyer's cunning smirk and whispered to Nussle, "They have resolved to avenge themselves by informing on me to my cousin. You will see, the seventy-five pounds is ours. Everything that is owed to us will be ours as well.''

MR. STARR AWAITED delivery of his seventy-five pounds at The Swan and Trumpet, where he and Nussle gathered together their belongings and packed them in a portmanteau. The stagecoach was due to arrive at the inn in less than half an hour.

Hurriedly, Nussle folded linens and cravats so that they would crease as little as possible. Every thirty seconds or so, he glanced at his pocket watch. Mr. Starr, meanwhile, was engaged in fondling miniatures, locks of hair, and other mementos given to him by the ladies of Nardingham. Then, having kissed each one in turn, he tossed them onto the bed for the chambermaid to find when he was gone. He was interrupted in this occupation by a knock at the door.

"Nussle, be so good as to let Mr. Aycock come in," said Mr. Starr.

Nussle answered the door in his most imposing manner. Seeing that he had opened the door to Miss Guggins, the farmer's daughter, Nussle did not disguise his disapproval. He announced unnecessarily but forcibly, "Miss Guggins, sir."

Smiling, Mr. Starr greeted her by taking both her hands in his and putting them to his lips, causing her to quiver. He peered at Nussle over her shoulder, wrinkling his handsome brow as if to say, "What are we to do with her?" He wished to spare her the mortification of being discovered in his bedchamber by Mr. Aycock. When Nussle answered him with a shrug, Mr. Starr turned to his visitor and said, "My dear young lady, you know you ought not to have come. What if you should be found here?"

"I care not!" she cried, and would have carried off this piece of theatrics very prettily except that she was obliged to sneeze. Mr. Starr had to endure a fit of her sneezes before he could scold her into leaving, but she was not to be got rid of.

"We plighted our troth, Ryder," she said. "Therefore, you cannot leave unless you take me with you."

"We did not plight our troth, Miss Guggins. I make it a point never to plight anything, least of all my troth. Had I gone back on this solemn vow, I should certainly have remembered. I cannot and will not take you with me. I cannot and will not take anybody, excepting Nussle, of course, who has been my rock since I was in leading-strings."

She gazed at him worshipfully. "I do not understand a word of what you have said, Ryder, but I do love to hear you talk. Your words are so pretty. Tell me more."

"I will tell you this, and plainly. You must go away now, like a good girl."

"We shall be married, and then I shall never leave you."

He rolled his eyes. "You must listen more carefully, dear girl. I said I cannot marry you."

"Oh, but you can and you will. I am quite determined that Papa will accept you, for I love you with all my heart." She punctuated this declaration with a ferocious sneeze.

When she had recovered, he said patiently, "It is not merely on your father's account, my dear, that I cannot marry you. It is quite simply out of the question."

"Why?"

"*Why?*"

"Yes, why?"

He turned to Nussle. "Why can I not marry the young lady, Nussle?"

Without blinking, Nussle replied, "On account of the other young lady, sir."

Mr. Starr cocked an eyebrow. "Which other young lady?"

"The *other* young lady, the one you have vowed never to forget."

"Exactly so, Nussle. Good of you to remind me." Gravely, he took Miss Guggins's hand and said, "There was once a young lady whom I loved violently and vowed never to forget."

"Why did you not marry her?"

"Why did I not marry her, Nussle?"

"Because she died, sir."

"Exactly so. She died, and with her died my power to love another. I may never marry, not even you, my dear. Is that not correct, Nussle?"

While Nussle supplied the confirmation, Miss Guggins lamented, "Oh, that is such a beautiful story, Ryder. You ought to have told me before. I should not have pressed you with marriage if I had known."

After throwing a nod of thanks to Nussle, Mr. Starr took hold of the young lady's shoulders and steered her towards the door, but before she could be urged out of it, he was stopped by the sound of another knock. Instantly, his eyes met Nussle's. While the servant stood at the door, hand on the knob, awaiting the signal to open, the master bustled the farmer's daughter into a small room off the bedchamber. When he had closed the door and arranged his person and dignity, he gestured to Nussle to admit the new visitor.

Nussle opened the door to discover, not Mr. Aycock, as was expected, but Mrs. Aycock, who regarded Mr. Starr through lowered lashes and simpered, "You sly dog, thinking you could skulk away without my knowing. Why, I know everything that transpires in Nardingham!" She approached so close to him that he was nearly overpowered by her scent.

"You cannot stay, Alicia," he said. "I expect a visitor."

"What of that? I've come to kiss you farewell."

"That is kind of you, but entirely unnecessary. You had better go at once."

"Yes, Ryder, my love, whatever you wish, but not until I have had my kiss." On that, she wrapped herself about him and held fast to his lips. When she released him, he gasped for air.

"Will you go now?" he said hoarsely.

"I suppose I must, my dearest one." He exhaled and escorted her swiftly to the door, but upon opening it a crack, he saw Mr. Aycock approaching along the corridor and quickly closed it again. Leaning against it and loosening his cravat a trifle at the neck, he said, "You cannot go."

"I knew you would be unable to part with me," she said, exulting, "after what just passed between us. You felt it as I did, the overpowering sensation, the pounding in the heart. It cannot be repressed, you are compelled to have more. Never mind, you sly dog. I cannot withstand your impetuosity. If you insist on having your wicked will of me, I am too weak to resist."

"Perhaps we ought to discuss the matter further—in the ante-room." Gesturing to Nussle to guard the door once again, he secreted the lady in the same room as Miss Guggins.

After a second's pause, during which he smoothed his cravat, he affixed a smile to his lips. At the sound of the knock, he gestured to Nussle to open the door.

Mr. Aycock stepped inside, saying, "I have brought the, um, money you require," and handed him a small bean sack full of coins and notes. "It is all there," said the lawyer. "However, you may wish to, um, count it."

The sound of a crash, a cry and a sneeze emanated from the ante-room.

To distract Mr. Aycock, whose attention had been caught by the noise, Mr. Starr smiled, patted him on the back and encouraged him to move toward the door. "As you are an honourable gentleman, and as my good friends in Nardingham are all honourable gentlemen," he said, "I shall not be required to count it. And now I bid you goodbye and good fortune."

Mr. Aycock was stopped in his progress out the door by the clamour of voices raised in dispute. As they came from the ante-room, he fixed his eyes in that direction.

"It is nothing," said Mr. Starr smoothly, "merely the chambermaid setting things in order."

"I believe I heard more than one, um, lady's voice," said Mr. Aycock. Then, summoning his resolve, he added, "Mr. Starr, you took your solemn oath you would leave without meeting any of the, um, ladies."

Seeing that the lawyer was not to be talked out of believing what he had heard with his own ears, Mr. Starr smiled modestly and confessed, "You are very astute, Mr. Aycock. There is indeed more than one lady in the other chamber."

"Who are they, sir?"

"Who are they?" Mr. Starr repeated.

"That is what I, um, said. Who are they?"

"Who are they, Nussle?"

Nussle replied without blinking, "They are two respectable ladies of unassailable virtue and reputation."

"There you have it," Mr. Starr said. "That is exactly who they are."

"I demand to know their names," shouted the lawyer.

Luckily, the argument in the ante-room had reached such a pitch that the lawyer's shout was scarcely noticeable.

Mr. Starr shook his head. "Do not ask me their names," he said.

Fixing him with a stern eye, the lawyer demanded, "And why should I not ask their, um, names?"

With a rueful smile, Mr. Starr looked him full in the face. For an instant, a flicker of compassion lit his expression. "Believe me," he said, "it is better that you do not know."

The lawyer met his look with scepticism. Then, seeing something in Mr. Starr's eyes that took him aback, he thought better of his demand. He replaced his hat on his head, turned on his heel and silently went away.

Mr. Starr watched him go. Then he whispered passionately, "Damn, Nussle! Men are nothing but fools and knaves, and women are not a great deal better!"

"Yes, sir," Nussle said. It was the first time in many a day that he had heard Master Ryder utter a sentiment with which he could wholly agree.

But not for long did Mr. Starr dwell on the piteous state of the human condition. The rumble of coach wheels was heard in the courtyard below. While the ladies howled, shrieked and sneezed at one another in the ante-room, he and Nussle took up their portmanteaus, descended the stairs and climbed aboard the coach, setting out for fresh woods and pastures new.

TWO: The Mysterious Benefactor

AURORA VALENTIN SAT in the parlour with her father, the bishop of Sudsbury, endeavouring to persuade him to walk out with her. He had kept inside for months, since the sudden passing of Mrs. Valentin, claiming that his delicate constitution forbade the least touch of fresh air and sunshine. He shook his head with gloomy stubbornness as Aurora presented to him all the reasons why he ought to venture out of doors.

"I cannot budge from the palace," he said, sighing pathetically. "I am fatigued to death. Besides, there is so much to be done, so many affairs of the diocese to attend to. Your mother always assisted me, you know. I am quite lost without her."

Aurora knew very well how lost her father was. While she lived, her mother had done the bishop's work, and although she had never actually mounted the pulpit and delivered the Sunday sermon, she had composed it, rehearsed it with him and copied it out in large letters so that he might orate it without squinting.

Gently, Aurora took her father's hand and said, "If you recall, Mama walked out each and every day. She regarded walking as the chief means of achieving good health."

With a tear in his eye, Bishop Valentin said, "Yes, and much good it did her. She is dead, and I have nobody to tell me what is the right thing to do. Oh, Aurora, if only you would advise me about the charity school. What is to be done? Why do you deny me this small service? You never used to be so cruel."

Aurora bit her lip, repressing the powerful impulse to give in. She felt that the easiest course would be to do as she was bid. But she was determined not to do for her father what he could do for himself. Consequently, she forbore to take the easiest course. Instead, she said, "I believe I can guess the reason for your fidgets. You have an appointment you do not wish to keep."

Sighing, he replied, "I am to meet the choirmaster at the cathedral, and I do not know what to say to him. Your mother always met with the choirmaster. Perhaps, my dear, as I am poorly today, you would meet with him."

"Mr. Goldthwaite is a benevolent old gentleman. He would be greatly honoured by a visit from the bishop himself."

"Do you think so? He would not be disappointed?"

"And the walk to the cathedral would do you good."

"Oh, but there is a chill in the air. Your mother always said that May is the month of chills."

"But having foreseen the danger, you may take precautions. You will wear your greatcoat, gloves and broad brim. And you will stop on your way to call on Mrs. Dove. She will invite you inside and you will drink tea with her."

"I have been thinking I ought not to drink tea. Your mother suspected that my lethargy might be attributed to it."

"Perhaps Mrs. Dove will offer you a glass of hot negus instead. In any case, she is certain to supply you with the very thing to restore you, for she always wishes to please. And it is only a few steps from Dove Cottage to the cathedral."

"Yes, but Aurora, I have a great many letters to write. I cannot possibly go anywhere with so many letters to write, and I cannot possibly write them all. Indeed, I cannot write any of them. Your mother always oversaw the correspondence."

"What an excellent opportunity, Papa, to learn who has been writing to you all these years. And think of it, you will be able to write to them in answer."

He regarded her with horror. "I shouldn't have the least idea what to say."

"Once you have read their letters, you will know exactly what to reply."

"Your mother always said I was incapable of deciphering the chicken-scratching in a letter. That is why she was so obliging as to save me the trouble. She composed the replies as well."

"What you require, Papa, is a secretary—a man who will read your correspondence aloud to you when you cannot make it out and who will pen a fair copy of your reply." Aurora had been on the point of recommending that her father engage a domestic chaplain, but thought better of it. Her father might easily relinquish to a chaplain his diocesan responsibilities and powers. In such a case, a youthful cleric would merely replace her mother as bishop. A secretary, a gentleman who was not ordained, would be much safer.

"A secretary?" exclaimed the bishop. He put up his hand as if to stave off such an atrocity. "I cannot possibly engage a secretary."

"Why ever not?"

"Because he will fall in love with you and be forced to go away again."

Aurora laughed at this notion. "You flatter me, Papa. A secretary will be too busy assisting you to pay me any mind. And I shall be too busy with the affairs of the Samaritan Hospital to pay *him* any mind."

"Nevertheless, he will fall in love with you. My curates and chaplains always fell in love with you. Your mother was obliged to scold them and send them packing, and then she was obliged to take on their duties herself. She never complained, though I dare say she worked herself to an early grave."

"Is that why you think your curates and chaplains did not stay above a month? Because they fell in love with me?"

"That is the reason your mother gave for dismissing them, and I am sure she knew whereof she spoke, for you are very good-natured, my dear, and a fellow would have to be blind in both eyes and as insensible as stone not to notice."

Aurora refrained from enlightening her father as to the true circumstance that had driven a succession of unfortunate clergymen from their household: namely, her mother's wish to perform their duties. Smiling, she gave her father a kiss on the cheek and said, "You are too partial by half, and I thank you for it."

"Then you will write my letters?"

"No, but we shall speak with Mrs. Bludthorn, who recently advertised for a governess and was fortunate to have found a treasure. Mrs. Bludthorn will tell us how you may advertise for a secretary in the most discreet and effective manner."

"You are as stubborn as your mother."

"I hope so, Papa. I am doing my very best to be." She rose to kiss his brow.

When he replied with a profusion of sighs, Aurora pushed her stool a bit back from his chair and held his hand. "Papa," she said, "have you ever thought how much good you might do in the world?"

His eyebrows elevated. "Upon my word, do you think I might do good in the world?"

"Everybody can, but you especially, for as bishop, it is in your power to encourage young men to be ordained, to ordain them yourself, and to confirm the children. In short, you hold the future of English youth in your hand, and by both precept and example, may induce them to travel the road of right living."

He blanched. "The future of English youth—that is a heavy responsibility."

"Of course, with the assistance of a secretary, you will not feel its heaviness, only the satisfaction of having done what was asked of you and done it well. The secretary will see to the particulars, but your benevolence, your justice, will guide the performance. Oh, Papa, think of it. This work will return you the greatest of rewards!"

Still hesitant, he said, "Do you think so, my dear? I should not like to put myself to all the trouble for nothing."

"I promise you, it will not be for nothing. And what is more, you may perhaps do a world of good to the gentleman you engage as secretary. Perhaps he will be a young man, and you may, in some sort, act the part of a father to him."

This notion struck him profoundly. "I never had a son," he said, as though he had not previously noticed the fact.

She encouraged him with a nod.

With uncharacteristic force, the bishop stood and set his jaw. "We shall go and see Mrs. Bludthorn," he said, "and if she can transform my chicken-scratches into an advertisement, then perhaps she may succeed in finding me a secretary."

WHEN MAGNUS VALENTIN had ascended to the bishopric of Sudsbury, it was feared among the good folk of the sleepy cathedral town that his only child, Aurora, would favour her mother. As she perfectly resembled Mrs. Valentin in appearance, and as she was, like her mother, an heiress, it was natural to assume the girl would emulate her in other regards as well. Thus, before she gave any sign of sharing her mother's propensity to haggle or to experience virulent fits of holiness, Aurora was accorded the epithet Little Miss Bishop and eyed suspiciously as she rode her pony, skipped along the lanes, and purchased tarts with her own pin-money. But the townsfolk soon saw that young Aurora was as different from Mrs. Valentin as sunshine is from rain, and that whereas Big Mrs. Bishop boasted a sharp tongue and a horrendous piety, her daughter was fair of face, tender of heart and liberal of purse. So liberal was she, in fact, that some years after her come-out, she amazed the town by using a considerable portion of her fortune to establish the Samaritan Hospital, a safe retreat for the relief and reformation of wretched female outcasts from society.

Mrs. Valentin had scolded others so often and so unpleasantly on the subject of charity that it would have been the eighth wonder of the world if Aurora had not been infected with a propensity to do good works. Even more persuasive to Aurora, however, had been the plight of a young woman she had found on the High Street of Sudsbury, slumped against the door of the baker's shop, faint with illness and cold. The girl was younger than herself and, by her own tale, entirely without money, friends or resources. She had fled London, where she had been enticed from her family under promise of marriage and then deserted by her seducer. Her hope had been to escape prostitution, and it seemed likely she would indeed escape that fate, for starvation and exposure to the elements threatened to deny her the prospect of any life at all, let alone a life of vice. Aurora had taken the girl to the bishop's palace and persuaded her parents that, dirty and foul-smelling as she was, she deserved the very best bedchamber, a visit from the surgeon and the softest nightdress in her possession.

Not long after, though she had only just reached her majority, Aurora had boldly initiated the establishment of the hospital and the Ladies' Association that supported it. In this endeavour, she had enlisted the aid of her father's London solicitor, Mr. Benjamin Puissant. After receiving a visit from Aurora and hearing her earnest plea regarding the nature and purpose of the charity, Mr. Puissant had taken it upon himself to become its agent, so that while Aurora directed the daily activities of the Ladies' Association, all matters of a financial nature were carried out by him.

If Aurora's public passion was to advance the cause of the Samaritan Hospital, her private passion was to stir her father to an active life. She hoped to renew his health by distracting him from constant preoccupation with it. She could think of no better distraction than strenuous and worthwhile employment, which the office of bishop had certainly afforded her mother and gave every promise of affording the bishop himself.

Therefore, while she comforted her dear father in his bereavement and saw to his care, she was not willing to do as her mother had done and become the de facto bishop. It had been a first principle with her, from the time she was old enough to form an opinion regarding marriage in general and her parents' in particular, that if she wished to do or be something, she would not under any circumstance do it or be it in the name of somebody else. Unlike her mother, she did not choose to express her own gifts and ambitions by dominating those she loved.

She did resemble her mother in one respect, however—her ability to influence her father. Thus, the very next day after their conversation in the parlour, the bishop agreed to walk out with his daughter.

They strolled along the cobbled High Street, exciting the stares of the townsfolk, who had never before seen Bishop Valentin take the morning air. The townspeople soon recovered from their shock sufficiently to raise their caps, nod their heads and offer greetings.

Aurora was gratified beyond measure that she had been able to coax her father from the palace. Forgetting the solemnity that mourning imposed on her, she returned her neighbours' good-mornings with warm animation. Her forgetfulness did her credit in the eyes of the Sudsburians. The men speculated that some clever fellow would soon capture the delightful Little Miss Bishop's heart and carry her off. The women gave it as their opinion that the sweet child would be forced to marry beneath her, for they did not know where the man might be found who was half good enough for her. All agreed, however, that the sight of the bishop, looking pink-cheeked and ambulatory, and his daughter, fetching even in the most sombre black, was a veritable treat.

Their destination was the post office.

"I have never visited the post office," the bishop had protested earlier. "Your mother always saw to the posting of letters, and I expect she sent a servant on such errands."

"Mama often posted her own letters, Papa, for then she knew they had been properly sent. Moreover, she wished to have in hand all letters addressed to the palace as soon as the mail coach reached Sudsbury. I suspect that she also enjoyed the walk to the post office, for it is very agreeable. If you will accompany me on the walk, I shall post your letter for you."

Hearing that his wife had approved of such expeditions, the bishop had finally agreed to walk out. Now, as he strolled the High Street, he gradually forgot his previous reluctance to brave the spring air. Shyly he smiled, nodded to his neighbours, and complained only ten or eleven times of the May chill.

Soon they turned in to the post office, where they were greeted by the postmaster. Aurora posted the letter to the *Morning Chronicle* containing Bishop Valentin's advertisement for a secretary. Following that transaction, she was handed a letter from Benjamin Puissant, Esquire. Eagerly, she broke the seal and, opening the paper, read as follows:

My Dear Miss Valentin,
I send you a bank draft in the amount of seventeen pounds, which represents the proceeds of a money letter sent to me from the north of England, along with a brief note of instruction to the effect that the entire sum constitutes a donation to the Samaritan Hospital. Like the other letters sent to me in the same mysterious manner, this one bears an insignia in place of a signature. As before, I relay it to you for your inspection. I devoutly hope that in future your anonymous benefactor will enclose a farthing to guarantee the money's safe arrival. The post office is an excellent institution, but one cannot be too careful in this age of thievery and vice. I trust your father continues to bear up nobly under his bereavement, as he has an excellent daughter to console him and to see to his every wish. Convey to him, if you will, my very best wishes for his good health.

                    I am your most obedient servant,
                    Benjamin Puissant, Esq.

Aurora scarcely looked at the bank draft, so curious was she to see whether the insignia matched the one marking three previous donations forwarded to her by the London solicitor. And indeed, when she unfolded the letter, her eyes fell on a small five-pointed star. It was exactly like the others: somewhat tipped in an easterly direction, as though it found standing straight and tall a dead bore and preferred a more languid style of comportment.

At sight of the star, her fancy was stirred and questions teased her. Who was this benefactor? Was she acquainted with him? Or her? Why did the lady or gentleman wish to remain anonymous? How could she convey her profound gratitude and, more to the point, an accounting of the manner in which the money had been put to good use? And, if the benefactor were a gentleman and not a lady, was he married? Was he handsome?

Delicious though they were, such questions were unanswerable. Aurora could conclude only one thing for certain: if Chance should ever disclose the benefactor to her, she would know him for a soul mate. He would be unlike anybody she had ever met. His generosity, his constancy, his insistence upon anonymity, all attested to the fact that he was a gentleman of superior character.

She would have liked nothing better than to continue to let her fancy roam in this vein, to conjecture about the mysterious benefactor as she did every night before she fell asleep, but her father required her attention, asking, "You have received a letter, my dear?"

"Yes, I have. It is another gift to the hospital from our mysterious benefactor."

"I see. Well, I suppose when I begin to write letters, I will begin to receive letters in the post, as you do. One often finds, I think, that the letters one writes are answered, and then the answers must be answered."

"Papa, have you any notion as to the name of this benefactor of ours? Perhaps you have heard somebody evince a particular interest in the hospital?"

"No, my dear. As I have told you before, I cannot imagine who it might be or why he chooses to interest himself in your charity. Perhaps he is in love with you."

"Like your poor curates and chaplains?"

"Yes, and perhaps he wishes to curry favour with you."

She laughed. "If there were such a man and he did cherish such a preposterous notion, why would he disguise his identity? I cannot think well of him or return his regard unless I know who he is."

"Well, perhaps he means to tell you in due course."

"Perhaps it is not a *he* at all. Perhaps our benefactor is a benefactress."

"Impossible. Where would a female come by the wherewithal to aid your charity?"

"If by wherewithal you refer to money, I suppose that heiresses do exist. I am one myself, as was my mother, if you recollect. It was owing to the liberality of the terms of my inheritance that I was able to make the first offering for the establishment of the hospital."

"Oh, I had not thought of that. Yes, I suppose there might be another female such as yourself possessed of a fortune."

"And she might be willing to give a portion of it to charity, as I am."

"True, but I do not see that she would have it sent by way of a money letter. A money letter is a very complicated affair, requiring double postage for the enclosure. Your mother used to complain of it, and it sounds a dreadful business. I should sooner carry a parcel on the mail coach than attempt to send a money letter."

"You are right, Papa. Why should an heiress send a money letter? She would in all likelihood send a servant to deliver the funds to Mr. Puissant personally. If she were required to use the post for reasons of distance, she would most certainly have found the means to have her letter franked.''

"I dare say she would have.''

"Mr. Puissant says that this letter was sent from the north. The others have come from the west and south. I conclude, therefore, that the benefactor cannot possibly be a benefactress, for ladies do not move about so restlessly as gentlemen are wont to do. Moreover, ladies, especially ladies of fortune, go where it is fashionable to go. The north has never been fashionable, to my knowledge.''

"Your mother always liked to move about. She said that if she was forced to sit still for two minutes together, she would go distracted.''

"Do you think I am right, Papa, that the mysterious benefactor is a gentleman?''

"I think it very likely, my dear, unless, of course, it is a lady.''

She inhaled as she prepared to walk back to the palace on her father's arm. *A gentleman,* she thought. The benefactor must be a gentleman. All the evidence pointed to it. Perhaps she passed him on the High Street every day and did not know it. Perhaps she had never met him but was destined to do so. Perhaps he was as passionate about rendering service to the unfortunate as she was. Perhaps he was as passionate in a great many regards as she was. It could be that he was a gentleman of excellent learning and fine bearing, a handsome man, charming and interesting. Perhaps, when she studied the letter again in the privacy of her sitting-room, as she did all the others, she would discover a clue to his name.

THREE: Suspicion

WHILE SITTING in Child's in St. Paul's Churchyard, taking coffee and a cigar with his newspaper, Mr. Starr found his interest roused by an advertisement. The advertiser wished to engage a secretary—"a man of discretion and quiet habits to assist with correspondence and diocesan matters." The word that caught his attention was *diocesan*.

"It indicates," he informed Nussle, "that the advertisement has very likely been placed by a bishop."

Nussle replied, "Pardon my inquisitiveness, sir, but of what use is that to us?" Now that they had come to the last of the seventy-five pounds donated by the gentlemen of Nardingham, he wished to know how the young master intended that they should live. The inelegant rumblings of his stomach told him they had better devise an answer soon.

"I shall tell you what use that is to us, old friend. I intend to seek the position."

Over his nose, Nussle peered at Mr. Starr. "You?"

"And why not me?"

"Master Ryder, you are a gentleman. You cannot offer yourself for a secretary, nor for labour of any kind. It is not seemly."

"In our present straits, I should say I haven't much choice. Besides, the notion of earning my bread by industry and application appeals to me. Do you know, in America, even the upper classes labour. They believe it lends them strength of character."

"At the risk of overstepping, sir, permit me to observe that if strength of character be stubbornness, you are already too strong by half."

Mr. Starr laughed. "You are a never-ending source of delight, old friend. You preface each sentence with an apology and an obeisance to the superiority of my station and the inferiority of yours, and then you level a verbal facer at me."

Ignoring this aspersion, Nussle continued, "As to earning your bread, you simply have not the gift, if I may be so bold. A gentleman is born to be idle. That is how Nature in her wisdom ordained it. Those who are so benighted as to think otherwise, such as your Americans and your savages, may do as they please, but in England, it is Nature that rules."

"I know why you object. You think me incapable of performing honest labour. I assure you, I am as well able to earn my bread as you are. An Oxford scholar is equipped for any task, however trivial."

"It may be, sir, that you are able to perform labour as proficiently as a member of the lower orders, but you will give yourself away the instant you speak. I hope I do not offend when I say that, in all truth, you are exceedingly arrogant, Master Ryder. You shall be known instantly for a gentleman."

Mr. Starr raised his brows. "How could I possibly take offence at such a compliment, my friend? I am offended, however, that you underestimate my powers of impersonation. If I choose, I am capable of being the humblest of creatures."

"*Humble* is neither here nor there, Master Ryder. It is *hunger* we must think of. At this moment, I could make short work of a roasted joint, as could you, I expect."

"I expect there is a roasted joint to be found in a bishop's palace. The clergy employ some of the nation's most illustrious cooks."

Hungry though he was, Nussle shook his head. "Do not answer the advertisement, sir. It is well known that it is bad luck to come up against the Church."

"Not at all. It would be a great thing for us to attach ourselves to a cleric of high position. Think of the breath of scandal we might kick up. Think of the indignant letter he might write to my cousin. Lord Matchless may withstand the complaints of our good friends in Nardingham, but if there is one thing that must absolutely drive him to the wall, it is the condemnation of the Church."

Mr. Starr called for paper, quill and a pot of ink, which were set down in front of him in due course.

Nussle stayed his hand to observe, "I should be remiss in my duty, sir, if I did not confess to you in all candour that I do not like it."

Mr. Starr looked up from his work and smiled. "Of course you do not like it, old friend." He clapped him affectionately on the shoulder. "You never like my schemes. That is my assurance of success. If you liked this one, then we should be obliged to abandon it altogether."

MR. STARR presented himself at the bishop's palace in Sudsbury only to find the bishop had gone out.

"That is very odd," Mr. Starr said. "He particularly asked me to come to see him on this very day at this very time. Is that not so, Nussle?"

As ever, Nussle was ready with a confirmation.

"He is expected to return at any moment, sir," the housemaid apologized. She dipped several curtsies, shifted about on her feet and gave every indication of wishing to run away.

"Perhaps I may wait."

The housemaid did not know how to reply to this suggestion. At last, she ventured, "I shall go and ask Miss Bishop, that is to say, Miss Valentin, whether you may be permitted to wait."

While she disappeared down the darkly wainscotted corridor, Mr. Starr and Nussle inspected the hall. It was walled and floored in stone and looked to Mr. Starr as though it dated back to the fourteenth century. Happily, its great fireplace blazed hospitably, warming the cold stone and giving Mr. Starr reason to hope that he would be welcomed in the cathedral city.

The girl returned. "Miss Valentin begs you will come into the parlour."

"And my friend?"

She looked up at Nussle and instantly wilted under his contemptuous gaze. Robbed of speech, she put her fists to her mouth.

"I shall find my way to the kitchen," Nussle announced. "The kitchen will please me very well."

Mr. Starr followed the scurrying housemaid to the parlour. When the door opened and he stepped inside, he saw a young lady standing in front of a tall window. The light behind her heightened a fine profile. He stopped to observe her. Though she wore bombazine, which covered her neck and arms, it was clear she was an attractive young woman. The elegance of her bearing roused his admiration. Hearing him enter, she moved to greet him, and he saw for the first time her face in full. It was more than comely; it was intelligent, humorous and gentle and surrounded by dark curls swept up in the Grecian style. His enjoyment of her loveliness was so complete that he forgot for a moment his purpose in coming.

"I do not know what is keeping my father," she said in a voice that put him in mind of a tune played on a harp. "Ever since I introduced him to the walk to the post office, he has made it his habit to walk out every day. But he has never been so late in returning as this."

Mr. Starr congratulated himself on his good fortune. The bishop had a daughter, it seemed—an exquisite vision of a daughter. Clearly, his stay in Sudsbury was destined to be a charming one. He bowed and raised her hand to his lips. Moving close to her, he said, in distinctly amorous tones, "A great pleasure, Miss Valentin."

Slowly she pulled her hand away and regarded him with astonishment.

Too late was he aware that he had blundered. A prospective secretary ought never to greet the daughter of his prospective bishop in the manner of a flirt. What was he to do now?

"I expect there has been a misunderstanding, sir," she said crisply. "I thought you were Mr. Starr, the gentleman who was interested in seeking the position of secretary to my father."

"I am he," he said, "the very same."

Her soft brow furrowed in puzzlement. "You?"

He smiled. "You are surprised."

"Why, yes." She tore her eyes from his face. After a moment's hesitation, she said, "That coat you are wearing."

He looked down at his scarlet coat.

"It looks as fine as anything tailored in London," she said.

There was no use in trying to appear the humble secretary, he saw. Nussle had been right: he was incapable of acting the part. He was too forward to be taken for anything but a Town gentleman. His only recourse, therefore, was to stick as nearly as possible to the truth. Telling the truth was always dangerous, he knew, but it was a strata-gem that appealed to him by virtue of its novelty. Accord-ingly, he replied, "It *was* tailored in London. Do you like it?"

"I expect it was a gift from the gentleman who last en-gaged you."

"Not at all. I have all my coats tailored in Bond Street. That is to say, there was a time when my coats were tailored in Town. It has been some time since I have been fitted for a new one. This coat is somewhat out of fashion, I fear, but it will serve."

"You do not look like a secretary, Mr. Starr, if you will forgive my saying so."

He smiled into her earth brown eyes. "I could forgive anything you asked."

She blushed fiercely. "You do not speak like a secretary, either."

"It is true. I am a conceited, arrogant, impudent puppy. I beg your indulgence, Miss Valentin. I cannot help it."

"I do not understand."

"Alas, I was raised a gentleman and am therefore unfit for any useful employment save flirting. At the same time, I have not the blunt to live as a gentleman and am forced to get my bread by honest means."

"I fear you are a fribble, sir."

"Dear lady, you assume I am a fribble merely because I talk and dress like a fribble and because I have the address, manners and air of a fribble. The truth is I am a man who will make your father an excellent secretary. Why, I have committed to memory several of Fordyce's sermons. I read in a voice loud, slow and distinct. And I write in a very fair hand. Shall I write something for you?"

She frowned. His bantering tone, not to mention his smile, put her off.

When he saw that she was not amused by his quizzing, he tried again. "I shall give you a demonstration of my voice." He cleared his throat. Gesturing widely, he intoned, "'Let me see thy countenance, let me hear thy voice. For sweet is thy voice, and thy countenance is comely. My beloved is mine, and I am hers—'"

"You need not go on!" she cried.

"It is from the Scriptures—the Song of Solomon."

"I know it is from the Scriptures, but I do not wish to hear it just now."

He was struck by the distress that creased her lovely face. It occurred to him that the young lady had not been flirted with before and scarcely knew how to behave. His inconsequential nonsense had put her entirely out of countenance. She hadn't an inkling of how to give him a set-down or how to flirt with him in return. He was liking her better and better every minute.

"Mr. Starr," she said, calming herself, "perhaps it would be best if you did not wait for my father. I believe he had somebody older in mind for the position."

"He must engage me. I insist upon it."

Incredulous, she said, "I beg your pardon. What did you say?"

"I said he must engage me and only me, for, as I have told you, I shall make him an excellent secretary."

"Have you any experience?"

He drew so close that she was obliged to step back. "I confess, I have little experience as a secretary—none, if the truth be told. But I have much experience of the world, Miss Valentin. Unlike the generality of secretaries, and bishops, for that matter, I have not been sheltered from life's iniquitous aspects. It would be impossible for anybody to take advantage of your father's goodness if I were his secretary.

I should deal with the world, while he would be at liberty to deal with holy matters.''

She hugged her arms as though she had grown suddenly cold. He half smiled to see her avoid meeting his eyes.

''Who are you?'' she asked. ''Where have you come from?''

Her directness charmed him. Reminding himself to hold fast to the truth wherever he could, he replied, ''I am the nephew of Lord Matchless that was. He brought me to Broome Court in Worcestershire when I was a boy, and there I was educated until I was sent to university. My uncle was devoted to me, and I to him. Therefore, I left the university to assist him in the superintendence of his lands and tenants. It was his intention to leave me provided for so that I might live as a gentleman. Unfortunately, when he died and his will was read, it contained no mention of me. My cousin, the present Lord Matchless, chose to regard that omission as intentional. He cast me off without a farthing, and so I am, as you see before you, a man without any means of supporting himself except his wits and his character.''

''I do not doubt you are possessed of wit,'' she said. ''As to character, I'm afraid I find it difficult to credit. Mr. Starr, it grieves me to say what I have never said to another human creature—that not a single word you have uttered impresses me as either sincere or trustworthy.''

He smiled. She might be innocent in the ways of flirtation, but she understood human nature. She certainly understood *his* nature. Perversely, he liked that quality in her. In one short meeting, he had discovered more to admire in this young woman than he had found in ladies he had known a twelvemonth.

"Perhaps this will be of service to you," he said, handing her the letter written by the gentlemen of Nardingham, commending him on his estimable character.

Aurora read it and reread it with attention. Afterwards, she inspected his face, as though she could not reconcile the letter's contents with the man who stood before her. Abruptly, she returned the letter to him and walked to the window. She stood there, lost in thought.

Her stillness interested him. Never had he seen a woman, or a man, for that matter, remain so long engrossed in thinking. He approached very near. Too near, but he could not help it. He said quietly, "I do not know you well, Miss Valentin, but I suspect you are too wise to judge a man by outward appearances alone. And I suspect you are too kind to condemn a man solely because his manners are at fault."

When she turned suddenly to face him, he bent towards her and their noses nearly brushed. With considerable effort, he refrained from kissing her.

Swallowing, she moved so that a chair stood between them. "You need not explain anything to me, sir," she said. "It is not I who shall settle this matter, it is my father. He and he alone will decide."

He smiled, tempted to go to her and take up her small hand, which played anxiously with the black ribbon at her bodice. He did not follow her, however. Instead he said, "I suspect, Miss Valentin, that you have considerable influence with your father. Daughters always do. You may persuade him one way or another, if you so choose."

She said firmly, "I do not so choose."

"Then you will not tell him how much you dislike me?"

She flinched. "I never said I disliked you."

"You are too polite to say so. Unlike myself, you are blessed with superior manners. But it is true, is it not?"

For a lengthy moment, she stared into his eyes. "It is not that I dislike you, precisely," she said at last. "It is only that you are not at all what I imagined a secretary would be."

"Thank you. My tailor will be vastly relieved to hear it."

"Mr. Starr," she said earnestly, "I hope you know how to be serious."

"Miss Valentin," he said, amused, "I hope you know how to laugh."

He saw the protest forming on her lips, but before he had the pleasure of hearing it, the anxious housemaid entered to announce that the bishop had returned and would see Mr. Starr straight away. With a look of particularity that brought colour to her face, he bowed to her, then followed the servant out of the room.

AURORA SANK onto the dainty sofa, keenly sensible of the irony of her situation. It had been her first wish that her father should carry out his duties independent of her or of anyone else, that he should come to know the wise uses of power by relying on his own powers of decision, and that he should discover within himself the aptitude for fulfilling his responsibilities. Now, at the first opportunity he had been given to test his mettle, she was champing at the bit to make up his mind for him.

There was no doubt he would heed her if she ventured a recommendation on the matter of his secretary. Every atom in her told her to do just that. Impelled, she rose and went to the door. She put her hand on the knob and, in her imagination, saw herself imploring her father to engage anybody—young or old, large or small, clever or stupid, handsome or grotesque, clear-eyed or squinty—so long as the man was not Mr. Starr.

The recollection of the fellow's insolence made her cheeks hot. In the brief time she had spent in his company, she had known more uneasiness, more misgivings, than she had experienced in the whole of her twenty-one years. His silky charm, his unflappability, his ease of speech, and most of all his maddening smile, struck her as dangerous. He put her forcibly in mind of the gentlemen she had encountered at balls during the short and unsatisfactory Season she had spent in Town. Those gentlemen had also been handsome, engaging and witty, but they had been false to their very marrow, and so was Mr. Starr.

She ought not to have persisted in being polite to him, she told herself. She ought to have ordered him away, and she would have done, except that there had been a glow of mischief in his eye that had unsettled her. She had been so occupied with wondering whether he was truly as audacious as he seemed that she had given him the advantage. At that very moment, he was sitting with her father, pressing that advantage. If she was wholly at a loss when it came to such a sly fellow, her father would be even more so. It was her duty to rescue him before it was too late.

But her hand, which still grasped the knob of the door, would not move. The impulse to run to her father's assistance was counterbalanced by an impulse to respect his power to make his own decisions. If he decided in Mr. Starr's favour, that was his prerogative. If she detested that decision, that was her own.

Her hand fell away from the door, and she put it to her forehead. She was astonished at the thoughts that had possessed her. For the past several minutes, she had permitted her mind to be filled with suspicion. That was unlike her. She was accustomed to thinking charitably of all the world. Why could she not think charitably of Mr. Starr?

Chastened, she returned to the sofa and sat, determined not to leave that spot until she had restored herself to her usual tranquillity. No doubt she had reacted too strongly to the man's careless air. She had allowed herself to be repelled by his Town manners. No doubt he was everything Mr. Aycock and the other Nardingham gentlemen had represented him to be in their letter. No doubt he was a pitiable gentleman who had fallen on hard times. She had no actual reason to think otherwise. No reason at all, unless the knot she felt in her breast could be accounted a reason.

"PERHAPS I MIGHT READ a bit of correspondence to you?" Mr. Starr said to the bishop, who regarded him with awe. "Come and sit down, and you will hear what a splendid voice you will have at your disposal."

The bishop lowered himself into a tall, carved chair. Mr. Starr snatched a sheet of paper from the desk and commenced to read an account of the laundress's charges for the past quarter. When he had done, he enquired, "What do you think, sir? Is that not a voice perfectly suited to the reading of clerical correspondence?"

Overwhelmed by the energy and confidence of his visitor, the old man nodded weakly.

"And now, with your permission, I shall show you a sample of my hand." He moved papers about until he had located a blank sheet. Then, dipping the quill, he wrote his favourite verse from The Book of Job, to wit: "I caused the widow's heart to sing for joy." Putting the paper under the bishop's nose, he declared, "That is a fair hand, is it not? See how the *h* and *t* slant gracefully. See how the *s*'s are neatly formed."

Even if the bishop had been capable of speech, he would not have been able to deny that it was a very fair hand indeed.

"Fortunately, I am able to be at your service as of this very moment," said Mr. Starr. "We may begin work on the instant."

"Gracious me," said the bishop, putting his hand over his heart. The young man had so completely taken his breath away that he feared an attack of palpitations.

"Of course, I must make one stipulation, Bishop. I cannot possibly accept the position you so kindly offer unless I am able to obtain your promise of employment for my devoted travelling companion, Mr. Nussle."

The bishop grew pale. "Mr. Nussle?"

"Exactly so. You will want to look him over, no doubt." He went into the corridor and, finding the housemaid about her dusting, sent her in search of Mr. Nussle. Then he returned to the bishop and entertained him with recitations from the Psalms until Nussle was brought in.

"Here he is," said Mr. Starr when the imposing butler stood before them. "He is as industrious a fellow as you are like to meet with in this lax age."

"How do you do?" the bishop ventured.

"I do well enough," Nussle reported loftily.

"Perhaps you would like to employ Nussle in your stables," Mr. Starr suggested. "I trust you keep a carriage and several hunters."

Nussle bristled. "As Master Ryder well knows, I prefer to keep as far from the stables as it is possible to get. I cannot abide animals. They are dirty, ill-behaved and foolish. However, if it is your wish that I serve in the stables, I shall be only too happy to oblige. I believe I know my place, Bishop."

"If Nussle knows anything, Bishop, it is his place," Mr. Starr remarked. "Well, which is it to be—the stables or some other berth?"

When both men looked in his direction, the poor bishop shrank. Taking a breath for courage, he said, in a voice that was scarcely audible, "I fear it cannot be."

Mr. Starr smiled. "Of course it can be. You are a bishop. You can cause anything to be if you wish it."

"I do wish it," said the bishop sorrowfully. "Nothing should please me more than to take you both on, but it is impossible."

Mr. Starr, who had been certain his late exertions had met with success, looked puzzled. "Why is it impossible?"

"Because you are young and fine looking and will fall in love with my daughter."

Mr. Starr repressed a laugh. "I hasten to assure you, bishop, I shall do no such thing."

"You say so now, but, alas, you will fall in love with her, just as the curates and chaplains have done."

"Permit me to reassure you, sir. I shall not fall in love with her."

"You have met her. You have seen how pretty and good-natured she is. You will not be able to help yourself. And therefore I bid you good-day, sir."

"I shall not fall in love with her, Bishop! Tell him, Nussle. Tell him I may never fall in love again as long as I breathe this earthly air."

Nussle regarded his young master sharply and asserted, "He will never fall in love again as long as he breathes this earthly air."

"I cannot fall in love, you see. I was in love with a young lady who died. She took with her to the grave my capacity to love. Consequently, I shall give my heart to no woman." He bowed his head and folded his hands prayerfully.

This confession stirred the bishop, who rose and approached the young man. "I, too, have lost the love of my life," he confided. "Not five months ago, my wife passed on. I do not know how I have contrived to go on without her. Certainly I shall never love another."

"Exactly so," said Mr. Starr triumphantly.

"What was her name?" asked the bishop tenderly.

"Her name?"

"Your lady love. Perhaps you would be so good as to tell me her name."

"Of course, Bishop. Her name was... Nussle, tell the bishop her name."

Nussle sent him a look filled with daggers. "Of course, sir. Her name was Fontinella."

Mr. Starr winced. "Fontinella?"

"Ah, was she Italian?" asked the bishop.

"A dark-eyed beauty and a countess," Nussle offered.

"Thank you, Nussle," said Mr. Starr between his teeth. "You have been helpful enough. You have the bishop's permission to return to the kitchen."

Haughtily, Nussle took his leave. The bishop, who had been engrossed in inner debate, now turned to Mr. Starr. "Permit me to extend my condolences to you upon your grievous loss, my boy. If you were my son, I should do my utmost to console you, and I should allow you to console me. In fact, we should console each other."

Mr. Starr paused. The bishop wore a gentle expression which, recalled his uncle's so vividly that the glib words he was about to deliver died on his tongue.

The bishop, perceiving the young man's speechlessness, came to him, his eyes brimming with tears.

Awkward for perhaps the first time in his life, Mr. Starr wondered what to do. Slowly, reluctantly, he put his hand on the bishop's shoulder by way of comfort. Then, all at once, the bishop spread his arms, and, to his astonishment, Mr. Starr found himself in the old man's embrace.

FOUR: "I Know Why You Dislike Me"

AURORA BORE IT with noble fortitude when her father announced that he had engaged Mr. Starr as his secretary. She had schooled herself to expect the news. Moreover, she wished to suspend judgement on the gentleman, believing as she did that manners were not necessarily a true indication of one's character. Reprehensible though they were, Mr. Starr's manners might easily be ascribed to the education he had received as a gentleman of the Town. Under her father's pious tutelage, his manners would almost certainly improve.

With such reasoning, she was able to muster all the good will at her command, which was considerable, and tolerate the gentleman. She even chose a commodious, modern bedchamber for the new member of the bishop's household. And when the bishop himself suggested that his new secretary be permitted to join them at table, she made no objection.

"He is a gentleman, after all," her father pointed out. "He is a Matchless and ought not to be expected to sup belowstairs."

"If that is your wish," said Aurora as cheerfully as she could, "I shall certainly see to it, Papa." It cost her some effort to appear to welcome Mr. Starr at their table, but as her father did not remark on the tightness of her smile and lips, she congratulated herself on having behaved as she ought.

Now Aurora met Mr. Starr not only in the corridors of the palace, not only in the great hall as she was coming in and he was going out, not only in the bishop's chambers, but also in the breakfast parlour in the morning, the drawing-room at tea, the parlour at supper, and, on those occasions when they dined, in the dining parlour of an evening. In short, she saw a great deal of Mr. Starr, an eventuality she had not anticipated.

She also had not anticipated having to find a place in the palace for Mr. Nussle. It seemed to her that no position, however grand, would come up to his high standard. He had made his dislike of the animal kingdom manifestly clear throughout the household, so that Aurora felt it was very wrong to place him in the stables. Whatever he put his hand to belowstairs, he managed with efficiency and care, but he terrified the other servants with his lofty air, so that they scattered to the four winds whenever they heard his deliberate step. Uncertain as to what to do with the man, she finally hit on the idea of taking the matter up with Nussle himself.

When he was brought to her in her sitting-room, he stood by her embroidery screen, as stiff, dignified, and unsmiling as a pike. She wondered how to begin. Happily, he spared her the necessity.

"You will pardon my speaking out, miss, but it has not escaped my attention that the bishop's palace is lacking a butler. I believe a housemaid opened the door to Mr. Starr and myself when we first arrived. Since then, I have noticed that the butler's office is filled by whomsoever happens to be about. It is, if you will permit me to say so, a havey-cavey business."

Aurora smiled. She was amused by the man's haughtiness and his woeful attempts at humility. She replied, "It is true, the palace has no butler. That office was filled by my mother before she passed on.''

Nussle peered at her with one eyebrow raised. ''Impossible, miss. I hope I do not overstep myself when I say that a female cannot buttle.''

Laughing, Aurora said, ''My mother did not actually open the door or polish the silver, but she assumed those duties of a directive nature that a butler would ordinarily carry out. You see, my mother was an immensely capable woman.''

''She would have to be, in order to serve as butler.''

''Mr. Nussle,'' Aurora said softly, ''I am not my mother.''

He took in the implications of that gentle observation and concluded that the young miss was as sensible and amiable a female as he had been privileged to meet with in some years. ''May I offer myself as butler to your father's household?'' he said. ''I served Lord Matchless as butler for upwards of twenty years. I believe I shall be able to put things right in a very short space, if you will permit me.''

She rose and pressed her hands together with pleasure. It had been clear to her for some time that the palace required a butler, and Nussle was more capable and experienced than anyone in Sudsbury. Thinking it was providential that he had been led to the palace, she said, ''You may indeed be the bishop's butler. From everything I have seen thus far, I have no doubt you will do almost as well as my mother in that capacity. Only I beg you will do one thing more.''

By now he was so enchanted with his pretty-spoken new mistress that he would have promised to groom her mare had she asked. Fortunately, she had something less revolting in mind.

''Do you think you could refrain from frightening the other servants?''

His eyes widened. "I? Frighten the servants? I am certain I never frightened anyone in my life."

"Oh, Mr. Nussle, you frighten everybody. Indeed, you quite frighten me."

He straightened his shoulders. "I believe I know my place better than to frighten the daughter of a bishop."

"I do not say that you intend to frighten, only that you are very imposing, and I do fear the servants will be so afraid of you that they will go into hiding and you will not be able to direct the household as you would wish."

Pondering, he said, "I suppose I might smile more."

Here he showed his teeth in an outlandish approximation of a grin. Indeed, it might have been more frightening than his frown if it had not been so hilarious. She had no doubt it would, once it was got used to, render Mr. Nussle a good deal less terrifying. "That will do very well," she said. Wryly, she added, "Now, if you can only persuade Mr. Starr to smile *less*, we shall all get on famously."

Shaking his head, he sighed. "I confess, miss, there are times when I altogether despair of Master Ryder."

Aurora's curiosity was roused. "Do you disapprove of him?"

"It is not my place to disapprove of the execrable manners of my betters."

"You are very wise, Nussle."

"Thank you, miss." With sublime politeness, he excused himself, but stopped at the door to say, "May I speak openly, miss?"

"I have the impression, Nussle, that you always do."

"Yes, miss. What I wish to say, or rather, ask, is simply that you not judge Mr. Starr too severely. I have every hope that as an inmate of this house, he will soon show his true nature, which is not at all what you have seen."

Aurora was touched by this show of loyalty. Her impression that Nussle would prove an excellent butler was now confirmed. It also spoke well of Mr. Starr that a man who appeared to know him intimately was disposed to think well of him. "I quite agree with you," she said kindly. "It is essential to suspend judgement of our fellow human creatures and give them every opportunity to prove themselves worthy of our friendship and trust."

With more emotion than she had suspected he possessed, Nussle said, "He will prove himself worthy. At bottom, he is the worthiest of gentlemen. You will see."

IT SEEMED THAT Nussle's prediction would be borne out, for Mr. Starr comported himself very agreeably. In fact, in the course of the next two weeks, Aurora was pleased to see that he was not merely an addition to the household, but also an asset. His conversation was lively and amiable. His electric presence enlivened the parlours and corridors. He spared no effort in his devotion to the bishop. Best of all, in Aurora's view, he never permitted himself to assume any of the powers the bishop was eager to confer on anybody who would take them off his hands.

One afternoon at tea, nearly three weeks after Mr. Starr's arrival, the bishop said, "What a disagreeable letter we have received from the vicar of St. Cuthbert's. What is your opinion, Ryder?"

Aurora raised her brows to hear Mr. Starr addressed in such familiar fashion, but she said nothing.

Having thanked Aurora for filling his cup, Mr. Starr replied, "I believe the vicar made mention of the church roof. I believe he said it leaks."

"It leaks very badly, he says. It is impossible to worship of a rainy day, he says. He is full of complaints, it seems."

"We have had a great many rainy days of late, have we not?" said Mr. Starr.

"It seems to me . . ." the bishop began.

The other two waited for him to complete the sentence, but he could not.

"It seems to you, Bishop," Mr. Starr prompted. He took a slice of bread and butter from the tray and appeared not to notice the void in the conversation.

Thus encouraged, the bishop went on to say, "It seems to me that when a roof leaks, it may have to be repaired."

"Exactly so," said Mr. Starr.

Aurora had listened closely to this exchange. Mr. Starr's patience and restraint were commendable in her eyes. She began to feel a sense of gratitude towards him.

"What is your opinion, Aurora?"

"I agree with you, Papa."

"And with Ryder."

"Naturally. I agree with Mr. Starr as well," she said.

Mr. Starr looked at her, and for a moment, she thought she perceived a spark of the mischief that had rendered his eyes so disturbing the day they had met. But he soon turned away and helped himself to cake. Aurora expelled a breath of relief.

"I suppose the diocese may allocate funds to repair the roof," the bishop said.

"I shall consult the ledgers," said Mr. Starr. "And then I shall go and see the vicar to arrange the repairs."

"You will do all that?" asked the bishop.

Aurora interjected here, "That is why you engaged a secretary, Papa—to do all that."

"Yes, my dear, but I should not like Ryder to walk all the way to St. Cuthbert's. It is very damp in June, and if he should catch a cold and it should turn to a putrid cough and he should die from it, I should never forgive myself."

Mr. Starr gave her a look that seemed to say they shared the same gentle understanding of the bishop's alarms. At that moment, she thought more kindly towards him than she had imagined possible. To her father, she said, "Mr. Starr will take one of the horses or the donkey cart, Papa. Or, if it would put your mind at ease, he will take the carriage."

"Ah, my dear, you always know exactly what to do. It is such a comfort. Why, it was you who thought of my engaging a secretary to begin with. And now look at us. We are quite perfect, are we not?"

PERFECTION is one of those ideals that may have been conceived solely in order to be dashed. Or so Aurora conjectured the morning Mr. Starr knocked on the door of her sitting-room. It was a pretty, east-facing parlour, bare of ornament and trinkets except for piles of books and miniatures of her parents. The sunlight filtered through cream-coloured curtains framing high windows that looked out upon a deer park. In the distance, a herd of does grazed near a towering chestnut. Aurora could see that the charm of the room and its prospect struck Mr. Starr as soon as he entered. His evident admiration of her surroundings seemed to her to be one more piece of evidence in his favour.

"I have been searching the library for a book," he said in greeting. "The bishop advised me to look for it here, with you."

"Please come in. What is the book?"

He stepped inside and closed the door. *"Persuasion."*

She smiled. "Gracious, I did not think you were a reader of novels, Mr. Starr." She invited him to sit, which he did, in the chair nearest hers. While she rose and searched for the volume among her piles of books, she felt his eyes on her.

"Ordinarily, I am not a reader of novels," he said. "However, I have been invited to attend the Ladies' Book

Society this afternoon. The book the ladies have selected is a new one by the author of *Mansfield Park*."

"I expect I shall see you at Mrs. Bludthorn's later in the day. I am a member of the Society and am most anxious to hear what the ladies have to say. Here is the novel."

He took it from her hand. "You have read it?"

"More than once."

"Perhaps you will tell me something about it. I cannot hope to finish it by this afternoon and should value your opinion."

"It is the story of a man and a woman who loved each other when they were young. Now they meet again, only to discover that their feelings have not changed."

"I see. It is about love."

She coloured, and did not resume her seat on the sofa. "Yes, but it is concerned with important matters as well, not merely love."

"*Merely* love? I do not consider love unimportant. You ought not to, either."

Aurora always bristled at being told what she ought to think. Therefore, she said coolly, "I trust that in the next several weeks you will have the leisure to read the novel through, even though you cannot do so in time for the Ladies' Book Society." She saw that he had caught the note of pique in her voice.

He stood, ready to go. Then, as if an afterthought had struck him, he said, "You think me remiss, I dare say."

She regarded him in curiosity.

"I never thanked you."

"For what?"

"For saying nothing to your father. You might have told him you dislike me, but you did not, and for that, I, and my old friend Nussle, are most grateful."

She blushed. "I told you, sir, decisions of that kind rest entirely with my father."

He approached her, holding the book to his breast. "He would have sent me packing if you had advised it. You know he would."

She detected in his expression a hint of one of his infernal smiles. It occurred to her that what irritated her so acutely in Mr. Starr's presence was the sense that he was goading her, deliberately egging her on. He devised awkward topics of conversation in order that he might see her squirm. Very probably, he was one of those men who liked to mock, if not openly, then in secret. At the moment, Mr. Starr's mockery was manifest.

Determined not to be baited, she said, "You have thanked me and have obtained your book. There is no further reason for you to take up your time with visiting." She walked to the door and opened it wide for him.

The dismissal was so clear that he could scarcely refuse to quit the room. He went to the door and seemed about to leave her in peace when he paused. He declared, in the manner of a man suddenly seized with an inspiration, "I believe I know why you dislike me."

Exasperated, she said, "I do not dislike you!"

"Of course you do." His smile was crooked, curling more on the right than the left, and openly audacious. His expression, together with his insolence, made her neck grow hot and her forehead begin to pound.

"I will not be told how I feel," she flared at him. "How dare you presume to know what is in my heart!"

His cheerful smile would not go away, and neither would he. "It would be far better simply to tell the truth, Miss Valentin. As you are a bishop's daughter, I need not remind you of what the Scriptures say in regard to truth."

She ground her teeth. "Very well, Mr. Starr, as you insist upon hearing it, I dislike you! I dislike you heartily. From the moment I first set eyes upon you, you impressed me as the most conceited, arrogant, frivolous, artificial man I ever hope to meet. There, are you satisfied?"

It gave her a thrill of pleasure to see that he did not appear at all satisfied. If she had not known better, she would have thought his sensibilities had been wounded by her outburst. His expression was serious. He was silent so long that she flattered herself he had been rendered speechless. In another moment, she thought, he would relieve her of his presence.

But she was not to be let off so soon. He drew near, regarding her with an intentness she found impenetrable. In a low voice, he said, "Yes, I can see you dislike me."

She cried, "Why do you persist in making me say what can only give pain? Perhaps you are impervious to pain, Mr. Starr, but I find it highly distressing to be obliged to say such cruel things."

"I am not impervious to pain." His voice and expression remained stubbornly impassive, a contradiction of his words.

"Please, I implore you, do not say any more. Just leave me and we shall forget that this unfortunate conversation ever occurred."

He held her with scorching eyes for some time, but shaking off his gravity, he said, with a smile that struck her as forced, "I cannot do that. I am obliged to tell you why it is that you dislike me. I shall stay until I have done exactly that."

Helpless, she said, "Very well, let us be done with it. Why do you imagine I dislike you?"

His smile widened and he came so close to her that it took all her strength of will to stand her ground.

"Because you like me," he said.

Appalled, she said, "Because I *what?*" She could not tell which she found more infuriating: his impudence or the irony that diffused his handsome face.

"You like me," he repeated.

"I *dislike* you because I *like* you? I venture to say, Mr. Starr, that is the most unintelligible speech I have ever heard." She stepped away and he moved towards her, almost as though they performed the steps of an intricate dance.

"My logic is absolutely irrefutable. Permit me to elucidate."

She made as if to move away again but found herself held fast by his sudden grip on her arm. A little afraid, and a great deal amazed at his audacity, she met his eyes, vowing to herself that she would not allow him to intimidate her.

"It is very simple," he said. An edge of his former seriousness remained, though it was couched in a light and careless air that confused her. "There are certain ladies who cherish in their fancy an ideal of the gentleman who will capture their hearts and sweep them off to the enchanted land known to one and all as Connubial Bliss. They imagine these gentlemen will be paragons, not only wealthy and titled, but also brave, honourable, and true. All goes well with these ladies until one day they find that they have grown inordinately fond of a gentleman wholly unlike the man of their fancy—indeed, a gentleman whose position in Society renders him entirely unsuitable as a husband and who is so far from being a paragon that the best one can say of him is that he is a rogue and a devil. She is in it before she knows she has begun. By the time she realizes she is head over ears in love, it is too late to resist. But clearly, she cannot allow herself to love such a fellow, and so she deludes herself that she dislikes him. There, I have explained it splendidly. I cannot imagine why I did not think of it before.''

A thousand retorts leapt into her mind, and she even considered striking him. Then, dismayed by the violent emotion that he had roused in her, she closed her eyes a moment, breathed steadily, and, vowing he would never see how much he had incensed her, said, ''Please, let go of my arm, sir.''

When he glanced down at her arm, he started. She had the sudden impression he had not been aware that he held her so tightly or, indeed, that he held her at all. Slowly, he loosened his grasp. They both looked at her arm and saw the red marks of his fingers on her pale skin.

Something—she could not tell what—jolted him. The darkness of his expression made her think he might now say a great many things that were rough and rude. It surprised her to hear him say with concern, ''I have hurt you.''

She backed away from him.

''I did not mean to hurt you,'' he said in such a soft tone that she could almost think he meant it. After a pause and a curt bow, he turned and went away.

Aurora had found the room close and confining with him in it. Now that he was gone, it seemed the tightest and narrowest of places. It was too small to contain her outrage. The walls seemed to constrict. The window and its prospect were insufficient to allow her the space and light she needed to breathe. Air, she needed air. Seizing her straw bonnet, she fled, and did not stop running until she had made her way out of doors, traversed half the lawn, and collided with a man carrying a basket of radishes.

SMALL RED ORBS flew through the air and came to rest on the lawn. Aurora bent to retrieve them, apologizing breathlessly, ''I did not see you.''

"If you please, miss," Nussle said, "I shall see to the radishes. It is not seemly for you to bother about them."

Too distraught to protest, Aurora rose and permitted him to gather the scattered vegetables. She still shivered from her late encounter. Holding her arms tightly across her bosom, she watched the butler, wondering how he could profess loyalty to a man as insufferable, incorrigible, and infuriating as Mr. Starr.

He looked up and said, "Are you cold, miss? Shall I fetch you a shawl?"

"I am not cold, Nussle." It was clear by the expression he wore that he perceived her disquiet.

"You must come and sit, miss," he said. His voice was firm, grandfatherly. She permitted him to lead her to a marble bench shaded by a crab apple heavy with pink blooms. While she sat, he set his basket on the grass and stood straight and tall near the tree trunk.

"If you intend to faint, miss, I'd best go inside and fetch the vinaigrette."

Indignant, she said, "I shall not faint. I never faint."

He nodded. "In that event, I shall just wait until you are recovered."

"Thank you, Nussle. You are very kind. To speak the truth, I am surprised. I should not expect any consideration from a close acquaintance of Mr. Starr's. Indeed, I should expect nothing but effrontery and conceit!"

This flash of anger caused him to peer at her over his nose. "If I am not mistaken, Master Ryder has offended you."

"That news does not surprise you, I expect. I have no doubt you know he possesses a rare talent in that regard."

"As a rule, the ladies like him very well. They do not seem to object to offensive conduct as much as you do. Permit me to say, miss, I cannot help but admire your discernment. If

I were asked, which I have not been, I should be obliged to say the ladies like him overmuch."

Aurora noticed that her cheeks were wet. Removing a square of linen from her sleeve, she wiped the streaks away, irritated that that dreadful man had driven her to tears. She replied hotly, "Here before you sits one lady who does not like him overmuch, Mr. Nussle. At this moment, I think I could hate him. I do not like to hate anybody. I have never hated anybody in my entire life. But I cannot help myself. I hate Mr. Starr. Oh, it is hateful to be forced to hate another human creature." The tears began to stream again.

Uneasy at this display, Nussle took the liberty of seating himself next to her on the bench. "Now, now, miss," he repeated as though he knew not what else to say to quiet a weeping woman. "No need to overset yourself." Gingerly, he patted her free hand, which rested on the bench. "Mr. Starr may have behaved in a manner to offend, but I believe he did not mean it."

She treated him to a blazing look. "He did mean it! His intention was to see me fly into a passion. And I have given him the satisfaction of doing precisely as he wished. I shall never forgive myself, nor him."

A grimace crossed his face and for a time, Nussle regarded her in some uncertainty. Then, looking off into the distance, where the terrace lay, lined with potted junipers and leafing box woods, he said in his dignified way, "Do not be angry with him, if you can help it, miss. I know the difficulty. I have felt it many a time. He can put me out of temper in the blinking of an eye, but I know his heart is gentle. Of course, I would never say so to his face, for he is too sanguine by half and thinks far too well of himself. That is why I am obliged to sound the warning knell in his ears. But I always remember what he was as a boy, when he first came to Broome Court."

Her interest roused, Aurora waited to hear more.

"He was a lad of no more than seven years and as skittish as a kitten. His father—brother to my late Lord Matchless—was a gentleman with a propensity for sailing, racing and gaming. He was sadly sunk in debt when he drowned."

"Gracious! He drowned?"

"They all drowned—the father, the mother, the sisters—all except Master Ryder. When the yacht overturned, he might have drowned, too, but he caught on to a timber and floated in the bay for a day and a night, until rescued by a barge out of Portsmouth. At first, the poor lad said he wished he had drowned with the rest of them, but my late lord brought him round. It seemed he would never smile, but he did eventually, for his lordship."

The story powerfully affected Aurora, who could not hear of such calamitous events without wishing to assist the sufferer in some way. If Mr. Starr had still been the melancholy orphan Mr. Nussle had described, she would not have hesitated to offer her sympathy and assistance. But as he was now every inch a man, and a rascally one at that, and one who smiled at the least provocation, her sensations were not so charitable.

"The father left nothing for the boy, not a groat. It was the uncle who took him in, brought him up as his own son, sent him to university, and promised he would be provided for."

Aurora sighed. "Lord Matchless was a good, kind man."

"He was everything a father could be to a lad. We all of us at the Great House saw how he doted on him. And no wonder. Master Ryder was joy itself, and full of mischief. He made us all laugh, even myself, I confess. On many an occasion, I made so bold as to carry him piggy-back."

"You, Nussle?"

"As a rule I regard children in much the same manner as I regard four-legged creatures—nasty, filthy and mean. However, Master Ryder was different. I cannot explain it, but so it was. When my lord looked at him, it was as if a sunbeam was smiling at a tulip, and Master Ryder, in his turn, was devoted to my old lord. Even as a boy, he had a heart as loyal and tender as anything I have ever witnessed in all my years on this good green earth. Unfortunately, the present lord is cut from a different bolt of cloth entirely. I never speak ill of my betters, but a more sullen, hangdog fellow I have never set eyes on and never hope to. He knew it was his father's wish to provide for Master Ryder, but pretended otherwise. You see, my old lord promised to leave a will stating his intention, but one was never found." Here, he looked about him to see whether anybody might be listening. Dropping his voice, he confided, "I am not one to speak gossip, miss, but it is my belief, and the belief of many others at Broome Court, that the young lord has purloined the will. By now, he has surely burnt it to ashes."

Incensed at this baseness, Aurora cried, "That is unconscionable! But has Mr. Starr no legal recourse?"

"None without a will, or at any rate, a codicil. There is nothing he can do, though myself and Cook and all of us downstairs at the Great House would swear before any judge that the old lord meant to provide for Master Ryder."

"Thank you, Nussle. I begin to see that Mr. Starr's extraordinary behaviour may in some sort be attributed to his unjust treatment at the hands of his cousin."

Relieved, Nussle said, "That is what I hoped you would say, miss. You will pardon my making an allusion of a personal nature, but I have observed that you possess a kind heart and, from what I have observed and what the servants at the palace say, you are not quick to condemn. If Master Ryder has been reduced to lying and trickery to make his way in the world, it is no more than you will be able to comprehend. He would not have done it had he not been forced to.''

''Lying and trickery?'' The words hit her like a lightning bolt.

Hearing his words repeated, Mr. Nussle went white. ''I beg pardon, Miss. I misspoke!''

Though Aurora could see he was horrified at what he had let slip, she could not let the matter drop. ''You said 'lying and trickery.' What did you mean?''

Rising and backing away, he arranged his dignity as best he could. ''If I have said more than I ought, I do earnestly beg pardon, miss. I should be sorry, very sorry indeed, to be turned out of my position or to cause Master Ryder to be turned out of his because I overstepped my station.''

Aurora saw that though he struggled to conceal it, he evidently felt a good deal of emotion. She responded with heartfelt compassion and went to him, saying, ''I promise you, I shall repeat nothing of what you told me. If Mr. Starr learns of it, it shall not be from my lips.''

As he was unable to express his gratitude in words, he bowed and strove manfully to quell his distress.

It would be wrong, Aurora told herself, to press him on the subject of Mr. Starr's ''lying and trickery,'' and not for the world would she cause the good man any more anguish than he was already suffering. At the same time, she was so alive with curiosity that it was all she could do to refrain from showering him with questions. To make certain that she would not be tempted to question him, she took her leave and returned to her sitting-room.

To her delight, the room had been restored to its former commodiousness. The walls no longer constricted. There was plenty of air, plenty of sunshine. One could breathe as easily as one wished. One could even twirl about and perform a little dance, which Aurora proceeded to do. The thundercloud had lifted, and all she could think was that she had not been wrong about Mr. Starr. Her instinct about him had been as accurate as an arrow piercing the bull's-eye. She ought to have trusted that instinct from the first. Certainly, she would trust it now. She swirled in a graceful pirouette and then another. Oh, how delicious it was to be right!

Her task now was to find what proof she could of Mr. Starr's lying and trickery. Toward that end, she located her writing desk, sat with it in her lap and opened the top. The first thing that came to hand was a small paper containing a star that languished slightly to the right. Taking it out, she thought of the gentleman whose insignia it was. Whatever his name, whatever his reasons for making the Samaritan Hospital the beneficiary of his philanthropy, he was her model of a true gentleman.

Mr. Starr, on the other hand, was her model of a true blackguard. Tucking away the insignia, she removed paper, quill and ink. For the next several minutes, she paused to compose a few sentences in her head, then dipped her point and began. She spent the remainder of the afternoon at her writing, declining to attend the meeting of the Ladies' Book Society. By dusk, she had completed and copied out in a fair hand two lengthy letters of enquiry—one to Mr. Aycock of Nardingham, the other to Lord matchless of Broome Court.

FIVE: Persuasion

AS HE WALKED from the bishop's palace towards the residence of Mrs. Bludthorn, Mr. Starr congratulated himself. In a remarkably short time, he had ingratiated himself with the citizens of Sudsbury. The proof was the manner in which they now stopped to greet him as he made his way. When he achieved the High Street, the butcher came scurrying from his shop to ask whether he and the bishop had liked the joint of beef he had lately sent to the palace. The baker poked his head out of his fragrant shop to invite him to taste a bit of apple tart. And the candlestick maker treated him to a view of his new infant, who squalled and drooled with admirable vigour.

Moreover, Bishop Valentin had lost no time in apprising his good neighbours of the circumstances that had reduced his secretary to seeking paid employment. The entire town— nay, the entire county—knew that he had been born and raised a gentleman and would enjoy a high position in Society if only his dastardly cousin could be brought to do what was right. Hearing this woeful tale, the Sudsburians had instantly taken him to their collective bosom, not only because their hearts went out to a man who had suffered the rankest injustice at the hands of his closest blood relation, but also because they regarded him as lively, handsome, energetic and interesting. Thus, he was able to felicitate himself on having won over, in less than three weeks, those he meant to fleece.

Another cause for celebration was the certainty that his cousin would not be able to withstand the outcry he would soon hear from Sudsbury. He remembered very well how timid a bully Frederick Matchless had been as a boy. The least difficulty transformed him from a menacing, vindictive swaggerer to a cowering brute. The letters of complaint he would receive from the cathedral town and its bishop would persuade him once and for all that the Matchless name suffered untold damage while he continued to ignore Mr. Starr's claims. Mr. Starr sensed it in his blood—Sudsbury was the last town he would be obliged to quit in disgrace.

To add to his celebratory mood, he had just succeeded in keeping Miss Valentin from that afternoon's gathering of the Ladies' Book Society. He had calculated that the meeting would provide a most auspicious opportunity for advancing his views on charity in general and the Samaritan Hospital in particular, and he wished to capitalize on the trust and admiration he had won in Sudsbury by collecting a goodly sum from the ladies. He knew he would not be able to do so, however, if Miss Valentin were present. Her suspicion of him, ever at the ready, would be roused by his appeal to the ladies' generosity and would set her in opposition to his manoeuvres. She would do all that was possible to discourage the ladies from opening their purses and turning over their pin-money to a virtual stranger. Thus it was that he had manipulated her into a quarrel, one so acrimonious that she would certainly be too fatigued and too out of sorts for literary chatter. The quarrel he had precipitated gave every promise of keeping Miss Valentin indoors for the rest of the day, if not the entire week, so furious was she with him.

Having all these causes for celebration, Mr. Starr could not help wonder why he did not feel more merry. Even in the bleakest of times, he was a man of sunny disposition. Though he had been exiled from Broome Court, the only home he had ever known, though he had been forced to earn his bread by subterfuge, though he had been hounded by a multitude of irate townsfolk and banished forever from their midst, he had always contrived to smile at his own absurdity and the world's, and to look forward to his next adventure with a sanguine heart. Why, then, did he now feel restless, uneasy, dissatisfied? Why could he not shake the sense that something just out of his range of vision was getting in the way of his complete pleasure?

The answer struck him suddenly as he turned from the High Street into Chipping Lane. Passing a broad-branched chestnut tree, he heard the warning note of a song thrush, and for no reason that he could think of, the image of Miss Valentin came into his head. Nothing about her dress or person that morning had escaped him—the soft complexion and rosy cheeks, their glow set off starkly by the black she wore; the earnest distress in her brown eyes; the energy and strength she radiated, drawing him near in spite of himself, so that he could inhale her scent.

Grimly, he recalled the marks his firm grip had impressed on her arm. His walk slowed as he recollected what had happened, how he had come close and seized her, wholly unaware of what he was doing. The infamous Ryder Starr, who never did anything that was not calculated, who prided himself on being able to keep his wits about him, even in the most trying circumstances, had in one foolish, careless moment acted purely on impulse.

An even greater source of irritation was the recollection of Miss Valentin's fiery contempt. Though he had wished her to confess aloud that she held him in dislike, and indeed had done everything in his power to provoke such an admission, her words had operated on him like salt on a wound. In his mind's eye he saw again the expression on her face. It seemed to say that she had been staggered to learn one human creature could be so cruel. Seeing that expression, he knew he had gone too far. His offence was beyond anything he had intended, beyond anything he could laugh off or regard as absurd or amusing. True, he had lately been reduced to flirting with women and cajoling them to part with their shillings and pennies, but he had never wished to harm any of them or give them cause to hate him. Least of all did he wish to harm Miss Valentin or cause her to hate him. In defiance of all logic, he wished he had been able to quarrel with her in a manner that left her liking him better instead of hating the very sight of him.

This impossible wish occupied his thoughts until he reached Mrs. Bludthorn's, where the Ladies' Book Society had gathered to welcome him. In the absence of Miss Valentin, who had sent a note expressing her regrets that she was too unwell to attend, the gathering consisted of eight ladies and their hostess. They ranged in age from twenty to sixty, in station from a poor parson's wife to the widow of a baron, and in appearance from short and square to tall and spindly. All regarded Mr. Starr with indulgent smiles and suppressed sighs.

They sat in Mrs. Bludthorn's best parlour, an elegant Georgian room painted pale green and furnished simply with gleaming mahogany chairs with maroon-and-white-striped cushions. Presiding over the meeting was the mistress of the house, who apologized to Mr. Starr for inviting him to a meeting for which he had to prepare by reading a book. She hoped he had not been put to too much trouble over it.

"Please, do not apologize," he replied. "As this estimable conclave calls itself the Ladies' Book Society, I guessed that I should be expected to peruse a book, and I had no

bjection to doing so. Indeed, I often read books, even
when I am not so fortunate as to be invited to attend a delightful afternoon such as this."

"Yes," said Mrs. Bludthorn, "but you no doubt read
books worthy of attention. I am afraid we have nothing to
offer today but a love story, and I know that gentlemen do
not read love stories. Gentlemen prefer history and moral
essays—works of import and weight."

He smiled. "You do not consider love a matter of import
and weight, I collect."

"It is well known, sir, that as love is a subject that interests ladies, it cannot be consequential."

Mr. Starr rose from his chair, giving the women a view of
masculine energy in its prime. While they caught their
breath, he said warmly, "Although I am a man, I am excessively interested in the subject of love. Perhaps such an
admission exposes me to the condemnation of my sex. So be
it. But I confess, I find a good deal of history and moraliz-
ing immensely tedious."

Emboldened by this confession, the ladies nodded their
concurrence.

"Stories of love," he went on, waxing eloquent, "go to
the very heart of our daily lives. What have we to do with
wars and conquerors and the like? What have we to do with
dry philosophy? Nothing! Our lives centre about those we
love and those who love us." Here he paused modestly. "At
least, that is my humble view of the matter."

"Mine, too!" said the parson's wife, as smitten by the
gentleman's handsome countenance and engaging smile as
by his vast wisdom.

Eagerly, the other ladies leaned forward. They stared at
him with varying degrees of fascination, while he strode up
and down, full of magnetic intensity.

"If there be those who disparage love," Mr. Starr said with fire, "I entreat you not to count me as one of them. Love succeeds better than anything I know in improving one's character, bringing out its excellence and lending it profundity. Nothing can awaken hitherto unplumbed depths of gratitude, admiration and tenderness so well as love."

The ladies stared, as though this last utterance had been made visible and now hovered on silken wings near the gentleman's lips.

Well satisfied with the effects of his speech thus far, Mr. Starr subtly steered his oratory towards the Samaritan Hospital, saying, "So many kinds of love inform our lives—the love between mother and child, for example." As all the ladies present were either mothers, daughters, or both, he felt certain of their sympathy.

"The love between the Creator and Creation," said the parson's wife reverently.

"The love between sisters," giggled the Dickery twins.

"The love between uncle and nephew," said Mrs. Bludthorn, with a significant look in Mr. Starr's direction.

He stopped, unsettled by this allusion to his uncle.

The lady explained, "The bishop has been so good as to tell us how fond you were of the late Lord Matchless, and he of you."

To his infinite irritation, Mr. Starr found himself overcome. He turned to the mantel to collect his emotions, only to realize that he was breathing too quickly to speak. The mention of his uncle had come like a sudden stab wound. The pain still managed to catch him unawares, even after all this time.

"What of the love between man and woman?" one of the ladies asked, endeavoring without success to turn the subject a little, so as to soothe Mr. Starr's evident distress.

"Or the love between husband and wife?" said another, hoping to draw the young man back into the discussion.

"They are the same thing," said the parson's wife.

"They are certainly not the same thing," the baron's widow contradicted.

The ladies then proceeded to debate the topic. In their heat, they forgot Mr. Starr, which gave him sufficient time to put thoughts of his uncle from his mind and to turn to the meeting again with a tolerable appearance of tranquillity.

"What do you think, Mr. Starr?" asked one of the ladies, after detailing the thrust of the dispute.

"I think the love between man and woman is wonderfully ennobling, and I have never heard of any rule that says marriage must put an end to it. I have even heard of certain cases in which marriage has enhanced love."

"Oh, Mr. Starr," the parson's wife burst out, "how you must feel the loss of your dear Fontinella!"

"Who?"

Mrs. Bludthorn elucidated. "The bishop has been so good as to tell us of your lady-love."

"Oh, yes, of course. Fontinella. I shall never forget her, to be sure."

"Was she very beautiful?"

"Oh, yes, very."

"Was she fair-haired?"

"Her hair was as fair as flax."

"The bishop had said she was dark," said the widow.

"She was!" he hastened to reply. "She was fair in a dark sort of way."

"Was she very accomplished?" asked the twins.

"Prodigiously. She sang and accompanied herself on the pianoforte, she painted screens, netted purses, had an excellent seat, all that sort of thing."

"How did she die?"

Because he did not have Nussle present to provide him with a properly heart-rending tale, he was required to fall back on his own resources. "Alas," he said, "she choked on a teacake."

The baron's widow replaced the cake she had taken from the tea table. The others followed suit. Mrs. Bludthorn whispered to the serving girl to remove the cake and bring a plate of plain bread and butter.

"She died in my arms," he said hoarsely, as though shaken with grief. Putting his hand to his brow, he bowed his head.

A hush of silent sympathy enveloped the parlour, until at last the baron's widow said triumphantly, "Ladies, I do believe Mr. Starr demonstrates to perfection what is meant by the love between man and woman!"

Mr. Starr, who had been waiting for just such an opening, now seized his opportunity. "How true, how true," he said, "but ennobling as is the love of man for woman and woman for man, there is a still a greater love."

The ladies waited with shining eyes to be enlightened.

"It is the love each of us demonstrates to our fellow—and our sister—creatures."

The ladies looked at one another.

"In other words," said Mr. Starr, "*charity*. No love is so excellent as the benefaction we display towards those less fortunate than ourselves, though they be unknown to us, dirty, unkempt, unwashed and despised."

"Oh, charity," said the Dickery twins, somewhat deflated by the sudden lofty turn the conversation had taken.

Mr. Starr had brought his listeners to the precipice. He now proceeded to push them over the edge. "Scripture says, 'Charity never faileth,' and truer words were never spoken. Charity never faileth to warm our hearts and instill us with that love that is the highest of all. Speaking for myself, I

now that whenever I contemplate the benevolence be-
towed upon destitute, ruined, wretched females by the
worthy institution known as the Samaritan Hospital, I am
illed with such spasms of love that . . ."

Here he stopped, for to his amazement, each of the ladies
had reached for her reticule and was rummaging inside for
whatever money she could discover. Mrs. Bludthorn,
meanwhile, had removed a China bowl from a nearby table
and proceeded to circulate it. In wonder, Mr. Starr watched
as the bowl was passed from lady to lady and each deposited a number of jingling, tinkling coins.

"What are you doing?" he asked.

Mrs. Bludthorn explained, "Why, sir, we are making our
donations to the Samaritan Hospital."

Mr. Starr had no mean opinion of his persuasive gifts, but
he could not quite believe that they were so great as to in-
spire such a swift and spontaneous show of generosity.
Abashed, he said, "You are excessively kind."

"No, no, it is you who are kind," said Mrs. Bludthorn.
'Miss Valentin generally speaks to us of the hospital at our
gatherings so that we may collect monies on its behalf. If
you had not spoken in her absence, I do not know what we
should have done."

"Miss Valentin speaks of the Samaritan Hospital?"

"You do not think it forward of her, I hope?" the parson's wife enquired anxiously. "Ordinarily, a lady would not
press such a subject so ardently, but as Miss Valentin established the hospital, I am sure it is proper for her to speak in
its favour."

Mr. Starr had to muster all his faculties to appear calm.
"I should not presume to think Miss Valentin forward," he
contrived to say with an approximation of ease. "However, I cannot help wondering why she does not employ Mr.
Puissant, the agent of the charity, to speak for it."

"Oh, she does," Mrs. Bludthorn assured him. "But as the hospital is located here in Sudsbury, and as Miss Valentin oversees its progress from day to day, she regards it as fitting to keep us apprised of its good works and permits us to do what we may to support them."

Carefully, Mr. Starr found his way back to his chair, striving manfully not to reel. As he sank into it, his hopes sank with him. The sleepy cathedral town that had a minute ago seemed the perfect means of bringing his grand plan to fruition had now turned out to be the last place on earth he ought to have been—the very site of the Samaritan Hospital. And the young lady in whose household he slept, ate and worked had turned out to be its principal. Closing his eyes, he addressed himself silently, "Ryder, my clever friend, you have walked with both feet into the lion's den, or, rather, the lioness's. What the deuce are you going to do now?"

SIX: Repairs at St. Cuthbert's

WHILE MR. STARR SET ABOUT extricating himself from the Ladies' Book Society, Aurora sat with her father. Suddenly a thought struck the bishop; his head snapped up and he said, "My dear, why are you not gone to Mrs. Bludthorn's? Are you unwell?"

Aurora was surprised to find that her change of plan had caught her father's notice. He was not in the habit of acknowledging anybody's blue devils but his own. She answered, "No, I am perfectly well."

Her father half woke the puss in his lap as he leaned forward to observe her. "Oh, Daughter, I can see by your pallor that you are ill. What if you should be gravely ill? What if you should be so ill that you do not recover? What if you should go to join your mother? What is to become of me with both of you gone?"

Tenderly, she smiled. "Do not fret, Papa. I have no intention of leaving your side."

He was not to be so easily reassured. "But why do you look so pale and peaked if you are not ill?"

Seeing that she could not successfully conceal her troubled mind, Aurora confessed, "It is Mr. Starr, Papa."

This admission alarmed him. "Good heavens, he has not fallen in love with you, I hope. Alas, it was what I feared most."

She smiled ruefully. "On the contrary. We have quarrelled."

He sat back in his chair and closed his eyes. "Thank heaven!"

Aurora was astonished. Her father was the most peace-loving creature she had ever known. "You are glad we have quarreled?"

"Oh, yes, I am vastly relieved. A quarrel is infinitely preferable to having him fall in love with you, as the others have done. In that event, I should have to give him his notice, and I should miss him dreadfully."

It grieved Aurora to hear her father express such fondness for a man she suspected of being a liar and a trickster. As gently as she could, she said, "I am afraid I cannot esteem Mr. Starr as you do."

"That is excellent. I could not wish for more, my dear, except your promise that you will not patch up the quarrel with him any time soon. I shall rest easier knowing the two of you hold each other in thorough dislike."

The irony of the situation amused her. Laughing a little, she replied, "I think *I* can safely promise that Mr. Starr and I shall be on the worst of terms for a very long time to come. There, do you feel easier now?"

"Infinitely, my dear. Thank you. You are the best daughter in the world."

For an instant, Aurora was tempted to tell her father all she suspected concerning his favourite, but she thought better of it. It was necessary to have proof of Mr. Starr's perfidy before accusing him. If she were too precipitous, she would likely find her father unreceptive. *Patience,* she told herself. *Patience.*

"You know, my dear," said the bishop pensively, "it occurs to me that Ryder has quarrelled with you on account of Fontinella."

"Fontinella, Papa? Is that a Portuguese dance?"

"It is the name of Ryder's lady-love."

Though she doubted Mr. Starr had ever confined himself to a single lady-love, Aurora pressed her lips together and resolved not to let slip a word of censure.

"The lady is dead, I regret to say, and the poor boy is quite bereft."

This piece of information went a long way towards melting Aurora's disapproval. "I am sorry that even such a man as Mr. Starr should suffer," she said, "but I do not see what that has to do with our quarrel."

"Well, Ryder is quite beside himself with grief, so much so that I fear when he sets eyes on a beautiful young lady such as yourself, he must either quarrel with her or fall in love. And as he has been blighted once already, the latter alternative is entirely out of the question, and so he quarrels instead, to protect his heart, you see."

This analysis caused Aurora's eyes to open wide. "Why, Papa, I do not believe I have ever heard you enquire so deeply into another's motives."

"It is Ryder's influence, I expect. He has a great experience of human nature. Why, only last week, the dean of Itchelsea would have given the living at Standing Poke to an undeserving clot, had Ryder not pointed out to me that the living was in my gift and not in the dean's at all. He immediately enquired into the dean's motives, asking what might have caused such usurpation of powers. When he consulted of the dean himself, Ryder discovered it was an honest blunder, for which Dean Craft was most apologetic."

Ryder, Ryder, Ryder. Aurora heard the name repeated with acute discomfort. She had vowed that hereafter she would see as little of the man as she could contrive, but that resolution did not bring her any peace. Her father, dear though he was, wounded her by repeating the name, and the only safety from the sound, short of putting her hands over her ears, was to excuse herself and take refuge in the quiet

of her sitting-room, which she did as soon as she was able.
For the first time in her life, she found it painful to be in her
father's company, and she placed the blame for this state of
affairs squarely at the door of Mr. Ryder Starr.

AS SOON AS MR. STARR returned to the palace, he sought
out Nussle, whom he found in the kitchen inspecting the
brandy to see whether any of the servants had got at it.
Nussle offered his young master a seat, which was refused,
as the gentleman preferred to pace. Seeing no reason for
both of them to wear themselves out with marching up and
down, Nussle seated himself.

"I shall quit Sudsbury at once," Mr. Starr declared.

Nussle's brows went up. "Have we finished our work here
so soon, sir?"

"I have no cause to stay. The Samaritan Hospital is located in Sudsbury, and Miss Valentin is its sponsor."

A cloud of doom crossed the butler's visage. "I knew it
was bad luck to go up against the Church. I hope I know my
place better than to throw past warnings in your teeth, sir,
but I did warn you."

Mr. Starr raked his hand through his rich brown locks. "I
had heard she was excessively charitable, but it never entered my mind that she had aught to do with the Samaritan
Hospital, *our* Samaritan Hospital."

"That is a most unfortunate development. However, I am
not surprised. The young lady is extraordinary in every
way."

"Yes, but that is neither here nor there. What is important is that I intend to bid you goodbye without delay." He
put out his hand toward the butler. "Come, let us shake
hands, old friend, and say farewell."

Nussle rose. "You mean to leave me behind, sir?"

"Yes, I do."

With a sniff and a raised chin, the butler enquired, "Are you displeased with my work, sir?"

"Of course not, you old rascal, but you are happy here, buttling for the bishop and terrorizing the under servants. I should be a cruel, selfish fellow indeed if I did not see that you belong here at the palace, where you may get your dinner regularly and do what you were born to do. Besides, the bishop and Miss Valentin need you. You have made yourself entirely indispensable to them, whereas I need to be off without any encumbrance."

"If I may be permitted to speak openly, sir, I believe I have assisted you out of more than one scrape. I have scarcely been an encumbrance."

Affectionately, Mr. Starr said, "You have been bang up to the mark." He then clapped the butler on the back and said, "Do not make it more difficult for me to leave you than it already is. There's a good fellow."

Straight as a ramrod, the butler announced, "If you go, then I go as well."

Mr. Starr rolled his eyes. "Why must you be so damnably loyal?"

"My late lord made me swear that I would look after you."

At this allusion, Mr. Starr lost patience. "He ought not to have done that, Nussle. He ought to have looked after me himself, by writing a proper will. He ought not to have heaped the responsibility on you."

The anger in Mr. Starr's tone caused the butler to grimace. "You cannot mean that," he said. "You know as well as I do that there *was* a proper will of some sort. It is that cousin of yours who has purloined it. By this time, he has no doubt destroyed it as well."

Gesturing in exasperation, Mr. Starr said, "I know nothing of the sort. A will, properly deposited with a lawyer, could not have been destroyed by anybody, not even so despicable a worm as my cousin Matchless. You know that as well as I."

Nussle bowed his head, repressing a tear. "I cannot explain how the will was purloined. I know only that I shall go with you, sir, wherever you go. Do not command me to stay, for I shall be obliged to disobey."

Mr. Starr remarked, "I sometimes wonder who it is that is master and who the servant here."

"I believe I know my place better than to indulge in such confusion, sir. If you are confused, I cannot help it."

Laughing heartily, Mr. Starr replied, "I wish you would not call me 'sir.' *Sir* is a term of respect, of which you have precious little, my friend."

"As you wish, sir."

"Now stop talking, Nussle, and let me think what is best to do. If I stay, I cannot pretend to have no interest in or knowledge of the hospital. I have already taken up an offering."

"Regrettable, if I may say so."

Mr. Starr fixed the butler with an ironic eye. "You always do say so, don't you, my friend? Be that as it may, however, my best course might well be simply to turn over the blunt to Miss Valentin, make what excuse I can for it, and find a new way to kick up a scandal that will blow as far as Broome Court."

"What sort of scandal?"

"It ought to be something that prompts the bishop to write to my cousin. A letter from the bishop himself will be most effective."

"If I may be so bold as to proffer a suggestion, Master Ryder, you might embezzle funds from the diocese."

"Yes, I might do so, but I would do so with impunity. The bishop is too innocent to notice. I should go undiscovered for half a century, I fear."

"Well, what if you were to take bribes? You might offer to use your influence with the bishop to obtain preferment for the highest bidder."

"Bribes! That is very pretty, Nussle. I always knew you had a larcenous soul. But I fear bribes would not achieve our end. You see, even if I were willing to accept a bribe, I should have the devil of a time scaring up a fellow to offer me one. There is a superfluity of honest clergymen about the county, and I do not think we could depend on any one of them to assist us."

"More's the pity."

"The truth is, Nussle, I do not fancy any scheme that has the potential to land me in jail. Call me coward if you will, but I should like to keep within the bounds of the law. And I think I may have a solution that will answer."

"You have that look in your eye, sir. I feel I shall not like this scheme."

"It must be wondrously excellent if you do not like it without having heard it. Shall I tell you what it is?"

"I suppose it is my duty to hear it, and I believe I know how to do my duty."

Rubbing his hands together, Mr. Starr declared, "I shall make Miss Valentin fall in love with me. I have already made a start by collecting funds for her hospital."

Nussle shook his head. "No, no, sir. It will not fadge."

Mr. Starr was warming to the scheme, however. "At first, I thought that my interest in the charity boded nothing but ill. Now I see I may use it to insinuate myself into her adorable heart."

Nussle regarded him bleakly. "I hope I do not overstep myself, sir, when I observe that the young lady detests the very sight of you."

"But why does she detest me? Ask yourself that."

"Because you behaved detestably towards her."

"Exactly so. I made her detest me, and I can just as easily make her love me. If anything will set the bishop to writing a letter to my cousin, that will. He will rail against the rogue who has made up to his daughter in the most deceitful manner. It will send my cousin straight to the wall."

The butler shook his head. "You will never succeed. With any other female in England you would, but not with Miss Valentin."

Mr. Starr's enthusiasm grew in proportion to Nussle's pessimism. "You also predicted I should never be able to pass myself off in the world as a man seeking honest employment. I proved you wrong then, I shall prove you wrong now."

"I do not know which is worse—for you to fail and go to all the trouble for nothing, or for you to succeed and break the poor young lady's heart."

Cocking a satiric eye at the butler, Mr. Starr said, "You are a rank sentimentalist, just as I always suspected. Are *you* in love with the lady?"

"I find her admirable in every way."

"Well, in point of fact, so do I. Therefore, I make this vow: she shall fall in love with me only a little. Before her heart can be irreparably broken, you and I will be long gone from Sudsbury and well on our way to collect our inheritance at Broome Court."

BY TAKING HER MEALS on a tray in her sitting-room and spending most of her waking hours on some call of charity or other, Aurora contrived to avoid Mr. Starr. To her regret, she was not able to avoid hearing him mentioned. Encountering Mrs. Bludthorn and the other ladies in the town, she heard repeatedly that at the Ladies' Book Society he had been wonderfully eloquent on the subject of the Samaritan Hospital. She was amazed to hear it, and even more amazed to hear that the ladies had thought nothing of entrusting him with their donations. It occurred to her that he might have pocketed the money. Indeed, she would almost have danced for joy to hear it, and to have her suspicions confirmed once and for all. It struck her as odd that a man like Mr. Starr would interest himself in philanthropy, of all things.

She was pondering that oddity when she turned into a corridor of the palace and came smack up against him. As it was a narrow, ancient corridor and both could not pass at the same time, he stood aside, flat against the dark wainscotting, so that she might be the first to proceed. With arctic dignity, she eased by him and would have hurried on her way without a word, but he stopped her.

"I have been meaning to give you something," he said.

After inspecting his face for the glimmer of a smile, she steeled herself to hear him out.

Silently, he withdrew from his coat a drawstring purse. Handing it to her, he said simply, "Donations for the Samaritan Hospital."

For a time, their eyes remained locked. What he was thinking behind his intent black eyes she could not begin to imagine.

"I know all about your speech to the Ladies' Book Society," she informed him.

"I was sure you would hear of it."

"And I know why you made it." She challenged him with a direct look.

"You know?"

It gratified her to see him lower his eyes and to note that his breath quickened. For a moment, he appeared unable to speak.

At last, he said grimly, "So you know everything. I expect you feel betrayed, and I cannot blame you. I am at a loss as to what to say to you, except that I am sorry to have injured you and your father."

"I should think you would be sorry. It was foolish of you to speak to the ladies merely in order to make up to me."

He looked at her, puzzled.

"Mr. Starr, you have no interest in the hospital. We both know it. You thought that by espousing my cause, you could persuade me to think better of you and thus mend the quarrel between us."

Slowly he smiled and exhaled in the manner of a man just pardoned from the hangman's noose. "How well you read me, Miss Valentin," he said smoothly. "I ought to have known I could not hoodwink so clever a lady as yourself."

"Not only can you not hoodwink me, but you cannot restore yourself to my good graces so easily as you might think. You will have to prove yourself if you hope to see our quarrel mended."

On that, she moved quickly down the corridor, but not so quickly that she missed hearing the parting words that trailed after her: "Prove myself is precisely what I mean to do!"

WHEN HE ENTERED the bishop's chambers, he was informed that he would be obliged to go to St. Cuthbert's at once—the very next day, in fact. There had been another letter from the vicar, again complaining of the hole in the roof. Bishop Valentin authorized Mr. Starr to see to the repairs himself and thus stem the tide of querulous missives issuing from that irksome parish. Mr. Starr promised to tend to the matter promptly. He looked forward to the journey out of Sudsbury; it would afford him the time he needed to plan his march on Miss Valentin's heart.

Although the bishop had exhorted him to ride, he elected to walk the three miles to St. Cuthbert's. The day was fine and he wished to enjoy the sunshine. He allayed as best he could the bishop's alarms regarding exposure to the elements and made his way on foot, whistling as he went.

The vicar of St. Cuthbert's nearly wept with thankfulness to hear that the diocese had at last come to his rescue. He recommended to Mr. Starr a local carpenter who was skilled in repairing roofs and much in need of employment. Raising his hat in farewell, Mr. Starr resumed his whistling and walked off in the direction of the cottage inhabited by Mr. Horner, his wife, and their fourteen children. It took him no more than half an hour to reach his destination, but what greeted him there put an end to his good cheer. The poverty of the hovel and its inmates appalled him. His heart went out to the good wife, who went about her cooking while suckling one child and shooing away the others who clung to her knees. Mr. Horner, meanwhile, slept on a rocking-chair, emitting snores which rivalled the cacophony produced by his offspring. As if that were not shock enough, Mr. Starr was then confronted with another, for Aurora emerged from a corner of the one-room cottage, holding in her arms a four-year-old child whose cheeks bulged with mumps.

"What are you doing here?" she asked, stopping at the sight of him. Clearly, Mr. Horner's humble cottage was the last place she had expected to see the late Lord Matchless's nephew.

"I have come to engage Mr. Horner's services in repairing the roof at St. Cuthbert's." Ryder did not ask what she was doing there. Mr. Horner's domicile, and the other impoverished houses nearby, had evidently been the object of her charity that day.

Aurora seemed to welcome his explanation. "Mrs. Horner," she said, setting down the child, who reached up her arms at once, wishing to be picked up again, "we must wake Mr. Horner. This gentleman is Mr. Starr, my father's secretary. He brings good news."

Mrs. Horner shrugged. "Mr. Horner don't like to be waked. I'll not do it, not for half a crown."

"Shall I write him a note, perhaps?" Mr. Starr enquired of Aurora, who seemed the authority to whom everyone else in that place deferred.

"He cannot read," she said. Then, leaning over the sleeping man, she shook him and said, "Please, wake up, Mr. Horner. There is good news to tell."

With his eyes closed, he batted her away.

Mr. Starr, wishing to prevent any inadvertent indignity to Aurora's person, strode to the rocking-chair and patted Mr. Horner's jowls smartly until the man stirred again. "Wake up," he said loudly, while the women and children looked on curiously. "I bring work—paid work."

Mr. Horner swore and wished him to the devil.

"Come, that is no way to greet a stranger who brings welcome tidings," said Mr. Starr amiably. Thereupon, he took Mr. Horner by the arms and pulled him to his feet. Taking a pitcher of water from the table, he poured it over the man's head.

Awake now, the carpenter rubbed his eyes. "Is't morning already?" he enquired.

"Permit me to introduce myself," said Mr. Starr. "I have been asked by bishop Valentin to find a carpenter to fix the roof at St. Cuthbert's. I am given to understand you are the man."

As the stranger's meaning dawned on him, Mr. Horner assumed a humble demeanour. "I am the carpenter hereabouts," he said, "and will do whatever your worship requires."

"Excellent. The first of your wages will be forthcoming this week if you can tear yourself from your rocking-chair long enough to commence fixing."

"Aye, sir, have no fear of that."

"I shall return tomorrow so that we may see to the materials."

"Aye, sir, I shall be awaitin' with two good hands ready and willin'." He gave a vast yawn and shook himself.

Pleased with the man's response, Mr. Starr now estimated what he might do from his own pocket to alleviate the family's situation. Because he was not to receive any wages until the end of the quarter, he was woefully short of funds. He did, however, possess six pounds and wished Mr. Horner to have five of them. Reaching into his pocket, he said, "We must see what we can do for you in the meanwhile."

Before he could withdraw the money, though, he felt a soft hand on his arm. He looked at the owner of that exquisite hand. Aurora's eyes appealed to him.

"Will you step outside a moment?" she asked. There was urgency in her voice.

"I shall be happy to step outside with you, Miss Valentin. Permit me to take care of a small matter here first."

Anxiously, she insisted, "This cannot wait. Will you step outside now?"

Her persistence amused him. Despite her softness and loveliness, Miss Valentin was possessed of a will of steel. But so was he, and he had no intention of moving until he had bestowed a gift of charity upon Mr. Horner. "As I have said," he replied silkily, "I shall be only too happy to be private with you in one moment."

Eyes flashing, she tightened her grip on his arm and pulled him towards the door. "It must be now!" she commanded.

When they stood outside, he glanced at her hand, which still held fast to his coat. "I wish you might have waited, Miss Valentin," he said. "I intended to give Mr. Horner a little something by way of assistance to his family."

"You were preparing to give him money, were you not?"

"I believe that is what I just said."

"Mr. Starr, I beg you not to give Mr. Horner money." Her rich brown eyes as well as her full lips implored him.

He arched his brows, half smiling at her impetuosity. "Why is it, pray tell me, that you are permitted to play Lady Bountiful while I am not to perform a single, tiny act of benevolence?"

Impatiently, she waved her hand. "Be as benevolent as you like, only do not give him money. You see, Mr. Horner is so unfortunate as to have a weakness for gin. He will spend any money you give him at the alehouse. If you truly wish to help his family, bring them food, clothing and other necessaries. That is what I have done, and I ask you, please, to consider doing likewise."

It was not often that Mr. Starr was inspired to give away five-sixths of his purse, and he was vexed that his rare gesture of generosity, instead of winning Miss Valentin's approval, had accomplished the opposite. Still, her appeal made good sense, and even if it had not, her expression, so heartfelt and alluring, must have persuaded him. He would not give Mr. Horner the money. But having disposed of that difficulty, he now had to decide what to do about Miss Valentin. It was too delicious a moment to let pass. He must somehow turn it to account.

Accordingly, he said, "As you have explained the nature of the situation so eloquently, I shall do as you ask."

Her relief was palpable. She inhaled, then let out her breath, so that her bosom rose and fell. Mr. Starr could have taken an oath that he detected the beginnings of a softening smile on her face. "Thank you," she said.

"Save your thanks, Miss Valentin," he said. "I should prefer some more tangible mark of gratitude."

She peered at him through narrowed eyes.

He nearly laughed to see how swiftly suspicion overtook her. Affecting shock, he said, "You do not suspect me, I hope, of an improper suggestion?"

She met his gaze head on, and it was as plain as a pikestaff that she was determined not to be the first to flinch.

SEVEN: Manners and Merriment

PINK WITH INDIGNATION, Aurora replied, "Your effrontery, Mr. Starr, knows no bounds. If it were anybody else, I should be shocked at the notion that I owed a debt of gratitude to a man for saving him from an act of consummate foolishness."

He was not visibly perturbed by this reproof. Bowing slightly, he said, "You may repay me by allowing me to assist you in your estimable charities. Like you, I wish to alleviate suffering among the less fortunate, wherever it may be found."

"I beg your pardon?" She did not believe her ears, nor a word of this professed devotion to good works.

"I am aware that you are energetic in the cause of charity. I ask only that I may be permitted to emulate you."

She did not know how to answer. If she gave him a setdown, she might deprive some worthy cause of an adherent, however hypocritical. If she did not give him a setdown, he would no doubt present her with another piece of impudence. At last, a thought struck her: a means of granting the gentleman's wish and, at the same time, of granting herself a modicum of gratification.

"Certainly, Mr. Starr," she said. "You may accompany me on my next visit to the Samaritan Hospital."

She flattered herself that he blanched at this suggestion, and it was no more than she had expected. The last thing Mr. Starr would relish was the prospect of seeing misery at firsthand; the sight would be sure to prick any conscience he possessed.

Before she could ascertain the degree of uneasiness she had provoked in him, he replied calmly, "I shall be honoured."

She very much doubted it, though she did not say so.

"And I should like to extend to you an invitation in return."

"What sort of invitation?"

"An invitation to visit your father in the bishop's chambers. You have not appeared there since my arrival. He has remarked on it and is sorry. He wishes you to see how well he gets on with the diocese's business."

This courtesy took the wind out of Aurora's sails. She was obliged to readjust her thoughts so as to respond with less rancour than she had evinced previously. "I have refrained from visiting until now because I wished to avoid interfering" was all she could think to say.

"Miss Valentin," he said quietly, "if it is my presence that keeps you away, I shall make certain to absent myself."

She hastened to answer, "Oh, no! I should like to see my father in his chambers, going about his business. I should like it very much. Whether or not you are there is a matter of complete indifference to me."

"I see," he replied, a hint of vexation in his tone. "Will you come tomorrow?"

She glanced at him closely. The subject served to remind her that, regardless of the gentleman's conduct towards herself, he had consistently behaved with the greatest care towards her father. And now that he had dropped his teasing manner and appeared quite genuine in his invitation, she was able to answer with tolerable civility, "Yes, I will come tomorrow."

The smile this elicited indicated naught but sincere satisfaction, as far as she could tell. Perhaps, she thought, the gentleman was not so lost to all sense of decorum as she had thought.

They took leave of the Horners and set forth along a footpath that wandered past St. Cuthbert's Churchyard and coursed through a pretty wood. They climbed a stile, then another, and at last attained the lane. On one side, the fields gently rolled and waved down to a green valley. On the other, a belt of trees wound into a double hedgerow. Aurora was aware, as they walked, that Mr. Starr was uncharacteristically taciturn, and as he was too young, healthy and fit to be winded from exertion, she remarked on his silence.

"I apologize for my rudeness," he said. "I have been preoccupied."

"The subject of your thoughts must be singularly important, to keep you so engrossed for nearly two miles."

"Yes, it is. I am considering what ought to be done about your situation."

Aurora felt the blood rush to her cheeks. "I do not have a situation," she replied.

"Oh, but you do, and a most lamentable one at that."

Her step quickened, along with her heartbeat. "Precisely what do you imagine to be my lamentable situation?"

He seemed to have no difficulty in keeping pace with her. "It pains me to say it, but you ought to be more merry."

She stopped walking, causing him to stop as well. The leaves of the hedgerow were thick beside them. Overhead, the sun shone hazily. "I am as merry as anybody in Sudsbury," she said with fire.

He shook his head. "You may be able, learned, charitable, good-hearted, quick-witted and beautiful, Miss Valentin, but you are not merry."

She bowed her head, flattered by what he had just said of her intelligence, kindness and beauty, but troubled by what he had added. For some time, she herself had been wondering if she were overly serious—if establishing a hospital at a young age, losing a mother and living with a clinging, dependent father had taken their toll on her disposition. Though she was far from eager to win the approval of such a man as Mr. Starr, she was too truthful to deny that his words might contain some justice. Nodding thoughtfully, she replied, "You may be right. Perhaps I am too serious."

With a short laugh of surprise and pleasure, he said, "I expected you to protest vehemently, or call me out, or at the very least, command me to keep my opinions to myself."

"I do not know you well, sir, but I know you will never keep your opinions to yourself."

This riposte appeared to amuse him. "I am far too lavish with my opinions, I own. It is what comes of associating with Mr. Nussle."

Aurora could not help smiling. A brief acquaintance with the butler had been sufficient to teach her that the man was nothing if not opinionated. "But," she said, "Mr. Nussle does not tease and provoke as you do."

"He never learned the technique. He has not had the advantage of an Oxford education. However, it is *you* we are speaking of now, you and your predicament. We really must do something about you, Miss Valentin."

"I do not see how. I am in mourning. It is not fitting to be merry."

"Society requires that you observe the public and private conventions of bereavement, but these consist principally of sombre dress and curtailed activity. Society does not require that you immolate yourself on the funeral pyre."

When she looked into his face, she saw that he was smiling, but contrary to her apprehension, he was not laughing at her. "Tell me, sir," she replied, "what does one do in order to improve one's degree of merriment? One imitates you, I suppose."

"I hope not. I am scarcely a model."

"You do not regard yourself as merry?"

He came close, and looking at her with a gravity not untinged with irony, he said, "I suppose to a young woman as upright and serious as yourself, I might appear to be merry, but I do not have to tell you that appearances may be deceiving."

"Then I am deceived, for you do appear to be the merriest gentleman alive."

"I may be arrogant, foolish, impudent and impolite, but I am not merry. You see, Miss Valentine, I too am in mourning."

A flush of sympathy crossed her face. "Of course," she said softly. "You are mourning your Fontinella. I quite understand."

Mr. Starr threw up his hands. "How is it that the entire world knows of my deuced Fontinella?"

"I beg your pardon if I have revived a painful topic. My father told me."

"Miss Valentin," he said irritably, "there is no Fontinella."

"Yes, I know. She is dead. My sincerest condolences."

His vexation was so extreme that he turned away, making a sound of disgust. "You do not understand," he said.

Aurora could see, though his back was to her, that he was agitated.

"I wish you to understand," he said. "When I leave this place, I wish to be able to say to myself that I told you the truth at least once, that there was at least one instance in which I behaved honourably. The truth, Miss Valentin, is

that there never was any Fontinella. She is an invention, a
fiction, a bold-faced lie.''

The fervour in his voice dismayed her. She walked round
him so that he could not avoid looking at her. "Why did you
invent her?''

"Your father would not have engaged me as his secretary
otherwise.''

"My father would have engaged you on the basis of your
merit. You need not have appealed to his sympathies.''

"That was not my intention. He wished to engage me, but
would not, for fear that I would fall in love with you. If I
did, he said, he would be obliged to turn me out. That is why
Fontinella was devised—to provide a reason why my heart
would be impervious to your manifold charms.''

Solemnly, Aurora pondered the confession she had just
heard. It did not surprise her to learn Mr. Starr had pre-
varicated in order to insinuate himself into the bishop's
good graces. It did surprise her, however, that he had told
her the truth. It did not surprise her to learn that her father
had feared his secretary would lose his heart to her. It did
surprise her, however, to find that Mr. Starr's lie did not
offend her. Indeed, it diverted her. She could not stop herself—she burst out laughing.

Mr. Starr regarded her in some perplexity. "I had not
thought you would heed my strictures on merriment quite
so soon.''

"Fontinella!" she cried through her laughter. "How absurd.''

"I beg your pardon," he said with an assumption of indignation. "It is wicked to laugh at the deceased. Have you
no sense of propriety?''

"No, I am far too merry!''

Laughing with her now, he said, "If I ever abandon the profession of secretary, I shall take up the teaching of merriment. I had no notion I was so accomplished in that line."

Recovering her dignity, Aurora said, "If your tale were not so ridiculous, Mr. Starr, I dare say I should be angry with you for imposing on us all so shamelessly."

"Then you are not angry with me? I am very glad."

She regarded him sceptically. "You are no such thing. Nothing gives you greater pleasure than making me angry with you." She glanced at him under her lashes to see how he would answer this directness.

He smiled knowingly. "You see through me, I fear."

"I have been waiting this entire two miles for you to make me angry. I cannot conceive what is delaying you. You had better hurry. We shall reach Sudsbury soon."

"You wait in vain. I have no wish to make you angry today. I much prefer to see you merry."

She suddenly found herself wishing to believe him. It was exhausting to be always suspecting a gentleman, wondering what his true motives were, and inventing retorts to quash his impudence. This amiability was ever so much nicer. For the first time in too long, she permitted herself to be easy in his company. So pleasant was the sensation that she permitted herself to smile.

"I very much liked laughing just now," she said. "It has been some while since I have laughed. I should like to learn to be merry. Perhaps my learning will help my father to be merry, too."

"I shall be only too happy to impart to you my vast store of knowledge on the subject," he replied, "but on one condition."

She sighed. Nothing, it seemed, was ever uncomplicated with Mr. Starr. He must always be teasing or debating or setting conditions. "What is it?" she asked, resigned to being on guard with him again.

"The condition is that you return the favour. I shall teach you the art of merriment. You shall teach me to improve my manners."

His stipulation was not as bad as she had anticipated. On the contrary, it was charming. Nevertheless, she felt it her duty to decline. "You see," she explained, "I make it a policy never to interfere in another's affairs."

He shook his head. "I had relied on your charitable inclinations. I did not think you would refuse to help me."

"It is not that I wish to refuse you. It is only that my mother was a very interfering sort and, though she meant well, she did much harm. I have vowed not to imitate her."

"So you say, but I know you have great compassion for females in need of help and have gone so far as to found the Samaritan Hospital for their sake. You did not balk at interfering there. Thus, I am obliged to conclude that your refusal is based on the circumstance of my belonging to the male half of the species."

She whirled on him with a protest on her lips, but the words died there. Heat rose to her cheeks as she realized that his gender accounted in large part for the excruciating uneasiness she often felt in his company. It was impossible not to notice that Mr. Starr was thoroughly masculine, especially at the present moment, when he gazed at her through velvet grey eyes.

Unhappily, she said, "You may be right. I may well harbour a certain prejudice against you because you are as you say, and quite rightly, and there is no justification for such a...but I have always believed that men and women are equally entitled, yet I confess to having established a hospital for females, and I cannot imagine why it is so difficult..."

She closed her eyes, mortified. Never in her life had she made such a muddle of a speech. Luckily, he did not appear to remark her confusion.

"If anybody knows how much I am in need of improvement, it is yourself. I entreat you, Miss Valentin, take pity on a truly desperate case."

Because he had overlooked her awkwardness, and because she did not wish to be accused of prejudice against the male sex, she relented. "Very well, Mr. Starr. I shall do my best to improve your manners."

Delighted, he took her by the hand and drew her from the lane through a break in the hedgerow and into a meadow by an elm. "Teach me now," he said.

Her hands on her hips, her tone sharp, she said, "The first lesson is that you must not be so impetuous, especially with the ladies. You ought to have asked me if I wished to pause a while under this tree."

"Would you have agreed?"

"Of course not."

"Then there was no point in my asking, was there?"

"You do not understand. If you wish to improve your manners, you must learn to consider the other person's feelings before your own."

He wrinkled his well-formed face. "What a very odd idea."

"It is not odd at all. It is the very foundation of civilization. Satisfactory relations cannot exist unless each considers the other's feelings. That is especially true of relations between the sexes."

"I am deeply grateful to learn this. You see, I had been taught that it was a lady's obligation to consider a gentleman's feelings and it was a gentleman's obligation to amuse himself."

Aurora shook her head in despair.

"This is vastly interesting, Miss Valentin. Pray continue."

"Well, to be perfectly truthful, sir, you must teach yourself not to stand so close."

"I had no idea this might be considered too close."

"I can feel your breath on my cheek as you speak." Suddenly self-conscious, she cleared her throat. "It is most disconcerting."

"I see," he said. Then, as though an inspiration had struck him, he moved a step away. "Is that better?"

"It is infinitely more polite."

"I was afraid you would think so. For myself, I find it far too distant. I liked it better the way we were." Here he stepped close to her again.

Gently, she corrected him. "You are not to consider what you like. You are to consider your companion's feelings. I can assure you, your companion feels a good deal easier if you do not stand so very close to her."

Reluctantly, he stepped back again. "I see that as my manners improve, my pleasure will decrease. It is not a great incentive to be polite, I fear."

"Your incentive must be the knowledge that you have made the world a little more pleasant."

"When a man is used to thinking only of himself, it is difficult for him to comprehend these complexities. How, for example, does one tell a young lady in a polite manner that one wishes to kiss her?"

"One does not tell her any such thing."

"But what if it is true and one does wish to kiss her?"

"One says nothing about it. One speaks only on unexceptionable topics, such as the weather or the surroundings."

"Do you advise me to practise hypocrisy, then?"

Colouring, Aurora said, "It is better to contain your impulses than to offend or distress another."

"But what if the lady would be offended and distressed by *not* being kissed?"

Her eyes went wide. "What do you mean?"

"I mean there are ladies who wish, nay, who expect a gentleman to kiss them. Indeed, if he neglects to express a wish to do so, they get on their high ropes and cut him dead."

Aurora regarded him helplessly. "I have nothing to teach you, Mr. Starr. You wish to know the logic of good manners, and if there is any, I can neither discover nor explain it. We had best continue our journey." She took a step toward the lane.

Impulsively, he reached out to detain her. Before he touched her, however, he withdrew the offending hand and put it behind him. Solemnly, he said with formal politeness, "Miss Valentin, I ask that you not take your leave at this time."

His effort to conduct himself according to her recent teachings was commendable. Therefore, she stopped.

"I am sorry to have proved such a dull pupil," he said. "You are quite right to give up on me. But it is my turn now. I must teach you merriment."

"Another time, perhaps. We ought to be on our road to Sudsbury now."

He placed himself in front of her, so that to reach the path, she would have been obliged to go round him. "The first rule of merriment," he said, "is to seize the moment."

She met his eyes and without enthusiasm said, "Very well, if I must be merry, then I must."

"The second rule of merriment is never to permit oneself to be offended. No matter what rude or ridiculous thing is said to you, you must treat it offhandedly."

She paused to consider this advice and concluded that it might well be sound. Responding to Mr. Starr with exasperation, reproofs and anger had done her no good. Perhaps offhandedness would yield greater satisfaction.

"If I may illustrate," he continued. "Suppose I were to tell you that I wished to kiss you. Not that I would dream of saying so! Thanks to you, I am far too polite now ever to make such a *faux pas*. Even if I did wish to kiss those delectable lips, even if I did wish to touch those satiny cheeks and that lush dark hair, I should never insult you by being so truthful. But imagine, for a moment, that I had not had the benefit of your instruction and was so lost to all sense of propriety as to say such a thing. What would you answer?"

"Nothing. I would not stay long enough to answer."

"Now that is precisely what I mean. You are too serious. You must learn to laugh, to treat such a suggestion as though it were the merest nonsense. You must not give impudent fellows the least hint that they have the power to throw you into a temper. In short, you must depress their impertinence instead of permitting it to put you in a state of high dudgeon."

Aurora listened attentively. There was nothing that intrigued her so much as learning a new way of dealing with a difficulty. "This is most enlightening," she said. "I should like to try it."

"Try it?"

"Yes. You must pretend you are a flirt and wish to kiss me."

"It will cost me considerable effort but I shall contrive it as best I can. Let me see. How shall I begin? Miss Valentin, you are the loveliest creature I have ever set eyes on."

She lowered her eyes and whispered, "Please recollect what I have said about standing so close, Mr. Starr."

"Oh, pardon." He stepped back. "I shall try once more. Miss Valentin, you are so lovely that I cannot resist the impulse to kiss you." He seized her hand and began nibbling at it.

She laughed playfully. "I dare not let you kiss me, sir. If I did, you would wish to kiss me again and then again, and I should find it tedious beyond bearing." Here she yawned.

He frowned in irritation. "Tedious?"

"I could not think what else to say. I thought 'tedious' might give just the right note of offence. Do you think the gentleman would continue to press me after such an offhanded speech as that?"

Rubbing his cheek as though it had been slapped, he said, "He would cease and desist at once, I can assure you. You are certainly an apt pupil."

Aurora said with a tinge of excitement in her voice, "I believe I shall soon have the knack of merriment. Do you think we might go on to the next rule?"

"As your progress is astounding, we may certainly continue. The next rule has to do with dancing." He took her by the waist. "We shall waltz, if you please."

She looked about the meadow, which was empty of all human life save themselves. They were surrounded by grasses and trees and, here and there, bluebells and lupins that tinted the meadow with soft patches of blue. No carts or pedestrians could be heard in the lane. Shyly, she said, "There is no music."

"Ah, but we have the songs of buntings, crickets, frogs and bees, not to mention myself." On that, he commenced to hum a tune and to dance, drawing her with him.

"I have never learned the waltz," she said, feeling that as awkward as her steps were, they were still not so troublesome as her feelings. Mr. Starr's charm was considerable.

She was aware of his nearness, aware of his firm hold on her waist.

"You must not resist, Miss Valentin. You must give yourself over to the flow of the dance. Imagine that there are violins, chandeliers, champagne, beautiful ladies and handsome gentlemen."

She held herself stiffly, thinking they ought to stop. "Perhaps this is sufficient merriment for one day," she said. "Perhaps we ought to be on our way again."

"You cannot leave the ballroom now," he cried, swirling her in a circle that dizzied her. "Your father is in raptures to see you dancing, and with such an excellent partner, too— a gentleman of noble bearing and refinement. There sits the bishop, between a duchess and a countess. They are plying him with all manner of good things to eat and drink, but nothing, of course, to afflict his delicate constitution. They amuse him with their gossip and, when he wonders whether his daughter's partner is in danger of falling in love with her, they cosset him out of his fidgets."

Aurora smiled. It gave her the greatest pleasure to imagine her father so happy and free of care.

"But enough of the bishop. Your thoughts must now turn to your partner."

"Who is my partner? I cannot imagine him." This was not precisely true, for in her fancy had formed the image of a man, one who was not only handsome and gallant but who also sent anonymous gifts of charity to the Samaritan Hospital.

"Your partner is someone who is striving manfully not to fall in love with you."

"What prevents him from doing so?"

He cleared his throat. "Well, that is difficult to explain."

"He has been warned off by my father, no doubt."

"Yes. No. Not exactly. You see, he must keep his feelings in check."

"Why?"

"Because he is a rogue and a devil and fears he may injure you."

"If he were truly a rogue and a devil, he would not care whether he injured me."

This gave him pause. "Very well, then. He must keep his feelings in check because he is the soul of politeness, a perfect hypocrite. He is growing quite miserable over it. That ought to please you."

The swaying and swirling made her heady. She scarcely knew what she was saying, so intoxicating was the movement of the dance, the warmth of the sunshine and the fragrance of the grass and flowers. "You are wrong, sir. I am not pleased to know he is miserable. I wish he were as merry as I."

"No, you do not, for if he were, he would confess his wish to kiss you, and then you would—with great merriment—inform him that kissing him would prove tedious, which would not only wound his puffed-up pride but might easily break his poor heart."

Aurora was now enjoying herself thoroughly, waltzing as though she had studied with a French dancing master since childhood. Lending herself to the movement, she replied, "You are mistaken if you think my partner has a heart. If he is a true gentleman of the Town, he is entirely free of such a sentimental impediment."

She opened her eyes to find him so close that she nearly brushed his chin. They stood still for an eternal second. Then, abruptly, he let her go, saying with an effort, "That is enough dancing, I think." After bowing elegantly, he turned on his heel and made for the lane.

Stunned, Aurora collected herself and hurried after him.

EIGHT: Mr. Starr's Secret

BEFORE HE HAD GOT very far, Mr. Starr slowed in his walk and endeavoured to collect his thoughts. He had caught himself just in time, before he had kissed her. Never had he come so close to throwing caution to the winds and giving in to his inclination; but then, never before had he experienced such a powerful inclination.

Why the bishop's daughter exercised such an effect on him he was at a loss to say. She was not the most beautiful woman he had ever met, and certainly she was not the most comfortable. In point of fact, she was singularly provoking, so much so that on occasion he felt his experience was no match for her innocence. A perfect example had occurred just moments ago, when he had encouraged her to be offhand in her response to flirtatious remarks. She had followed his instructions to the letter, saying blithely that his kisses would prove tedious, and to his consternation, the words had rankled. It occurred to him that success where Miss Valentin was concerned rarely yielded the promised satisfaction.

What would have satisfied him? Would he have preferred to hear her titter and simper in the manner of other young ladies? No, he would not have liked that at all. He valued her directness, her total lack of airs. He admired the manner in which she listened to his suggestions, even those he made in jest. She had the most astonishing faculty for finding something useful in them.

Would he have been satisfied if she had hung on his every utterance and gazed at him with lovesick eyes? Not precisely, but it would have been preferable to her indifference.

Would he have been satisfied if, when he had pretended to wish to kiss her, she had closed her eyes and turned up her lips to him? Yes. That would have been perfect.

All at once he recollected where he was and shook off these wayward thoughts. *You will not lose your heart to Miss Valentin,* he admonished himself. *Your purpose is to make her lose her heart to you.*

"Are you angry with me?" he heard her say softly. He felt her draw close to his side. "Perhaps what I said offended you."

He smiled. "That is a turnabout, is it not? Ordinarily, I am the one who offends you."

Judging by the expression she wore, she was not in a humour to banter. "When I spoke of my dance partner having no heart," she said, "I was speaking offhandedly, in the most general way, as you instructed. I did not mean to imply that *you* had no heart. I am certain you do. You must have one. I believe everybody, even the worst of us, has some sort of heart."

He laughed. "If you go on in this vein, Miss Valentin, I shall grow quite conceited."

As the implication of her words dawned on her, she coloured, much to his amusement. He anticipated that she would apologize again, but she surprised him by saying, "Mr. Starr, please do not think me presumptuous, but I have observed that at such times as these, one is apt to feel offended on very little provocation. One's sensibilities are acutely delicate."

He found her earnest expression captivating. "I haven't the least notion what you are talking about," he said.

"Nevertheless, you say it so charmingly that I am forced to agree."

"When I say 'such times as these,' I mean times of grief. You said earlier that you were in mourning, and as you were evidently not alluding to Fontinella, I conclude you were thinking of your uncle."

His laughter disappeared. "I believe we had better be on our way," he said tightly.

They resumed walking in the direction of Sudsbury.

After a silence, Aurora said, "Forgive me if I intrude upon your privacy, but I wish you to know that there are times when I am drinking tea or buying a ribbon or mounting my mare and, unaccountably, I recollect my mother's face or imagine I hear her voice. Just when I think I am in command of my emotions, I find I am not."

He glanced at her briefly, not without admiration. Miss Valentin was the only creature he knew who had put into words the very sensations he had experienced since the death of Lord Matchless.

"You must know," she said, "that your devotion to his lordship is spoken of widely in Sudsbury, as well as his devotion to you."

Ruefully, he shook his head. "It is true I was devoted to my uncle, but if you believe the regard was returned in equal measure, it can be for one reason only—you have been listening to Nussle. He would have it that my uncle was attached to me. As for myself, I am not convinced."

The look she gave him was heartfelt. It occurred to him that he might use her compassion at this moment to win her affection. Perversely, he could not do it. Instead, he remarked, "I piece it out this way: if my uncle had been as devoted to me as he professed, he would have kept his promise to provide for me. He would have made his will accordingly or added a codicil detailing his intention. I heard the will read; no mention was made of me. No codicil exists either.''

''Nussle says—''

''I know what Nussle says. He thinks there was a codicil or some other document and that my cousin contrived to steal and destroy it. However, I cannot credit it. You see, if the promised papers had been properly drawn up, my uncle would have deposited them with a lawyer. There would have been no opportunity for my cousin to purloin them. The fact that they were not so drawn up and deposited attests to my uncle's negligence, and his negligence attests to a want of true feeling. I am forced to conclude that my uncle did not value me. He merely fed on my attentions, companionship, loyalty and admiration. He regarded me in much the same way that he regarded Nussle, as a valued upper servant, except, you see, that he bequeathed to Nussle an annuity, whereas he did not give any thought whatever to my future.''

''That does not sound like the Lord Matchless I have heard described.''

''It is not the Lord Matchless I knew. But what else am I to think?''

She bowed her head. ''Oh, I do hope you are mistaken. I hope you will find that your uncle did value you.''

Mr. Starr considered his present position. It seemed to him that he had done more to ingratiate himself with Miss Valentin in the last minute than he had done in all his weeks in Sudsbury. If he were wise, he told himself, he would use this tale of woe to press his advantage. Unfortunately, he felt the situation too keenly to exploit it. The allusion to his uncle had revived feelings he had wished to suppress.

Aurora said, ''I hope your cousin will come round to seeing what is right and proper for him to do.''

He smiled humourlessly. "Have no fear. My cousin will come round. I intend to make certain he does."

"Mr. Starr," she said warmly, "if there is anything I can do to assist you in representing your cause to your cousin, anything at all, I hope you will not hesitate to call upon me."

Ryder Starr, a gentleman who never missed the least opportunity to laugh, now found himself in the most laughable of situations—the lady he intended to use to further his scheme had, albeit unwittingly, just granted him permission. It was a delicious irony, one he would ordinarily have tasted to the full. But at the moment he was not disposed to laugh. On the contrary, he would have vastly enjoyed putting his fist through a door.

THE NEXT MORNING, he determined that the better part of valour was to absent himself from the palace. Thus he would avoid meeting Aurora when she kept her promise to visit the bishop's chambers. If he allowed her the opportunity to level those earnest brown eyes at him, there was no telling what might happen to his plan or to him.

He thought of consulting Nussle, but dismissed the notion. The butler had predicted disaster and would like nothing better than to throw that prediction in his teeth. The only thing Mr. Starr detested more than being proved wrong was proving Nussle right.

Consequently, he left word for the bishop that he was taking the cart to St. Cuthbert's to see about repairing the church, and off he went. When he reached the High Street of Sudsbury, he drew the donkey to a stop and alighted, caught by the sudden notion of using the five pounds he had kept the day before to purchase provisions for the Horner family. After buying tea, mutton, salt pork, dried fish, butter, cheese, sugar and flour, he used what remained to acquire fabric, needles and thread, wool blankets, and candles.

Satisfied with having spent the last of his funds, he was on the point of remounting the cart when it occurred to him that he ought to have set aside something for the purchase of a spade, a hoe, seed and other necessaries so that Mrs. Horner might have a garden. It was June. If a garden were not planted immediately, it would not produce in time to be of benefit. Because he would not be paid his first quarter's salary for two months, it would do him no good to wait until his store of funds was replenished.

Happily, he recollected that he had authorization from the bishop to purchase materials to repair the church roof. He might use a few pence, he thought, to purchase the garden supplies. He would discuss the matter with the bishop when he returned to the palace. If for some reason the bishop did not approve the expenditure, Mr. Starr would repay the loan from his own pocket as soon as he was able, but he had every confidence that the charity would be approved, for the bishop was the most generous-hearted man he knew.

Soon Mr. Starr was warmly welcomed at the Horner cottage, and his bounteous gifts were exclaimed and wept over by a grateful mother, while her children introduced themselves to the cart donkey and fed it a bit of the sugar Mr. Starr had brought. By the time he had consulted with the carpenter, taken tea with the family, and received abundant thanks for his gifts, he was able to congratulate himself on being fully restored to his former self. The Ryder Starr who had been in danger of losing his heart the day before was in complete command of his emotions once more.

His resolution in regard to Miss Valentin was now stronger than ever. In two weeks' time he would win her affections and provoke an angry letter to his cousin from the bishop. In four weeks' time, he would arrive at Broome Court to collect his due. In six weeks' time—two months at the outside—he would have everything he wanted.

ALIVE WITH ANTICIPATION, Aurora knocked at the bishop's chambers. Hearing her father's "Enter," she pushed open the heavy oak door and looked about. The first thing she noticed was that Mr. Starr was not present. She felt a pang of disappointment.

"My dear, I am so glad you have come. Ryder has gone to St. Cuthbert's and I am dreadfully low."

She looked about, seeing signs everywhere of Mr. Starr's influence—a neat stack of letters to be answered, an answer in progress, an open ledger on a stand, full pots of ink, quills with their points mended and ready, a small table containing the bishop's favourite wine, favourite glass, miniatures of his wife and daughter, and a pitcher of fresh irises. The changes the secretary had wrought reflected a great deal of thought and care.

"Yes, it is too bad he is gone," she said. "It is not on my account, I hope."

Leading her to a high-backed throne of a chair, the bishop said, "I am certain it *is* on your account, my dear, for when two people quarrel, it is the most natural thing in the world for them to look to avoid each other's company."

Aurora smiled. "That may have been true formerly, Papa, but Mr. Starr and I are on better terms now."

"Ah, I am sorry to hear it."

"You cannot mean that."

"Oh, but I do. I should never be able to face your mother in Heaven if I allowed my secretary to fall in love with you. She prophesied that only calamity would result, and though I never had the courage to ask her for particulars, I have every confidence that she was right."

"Do not be alarmed, Papa. He is not in love with me. It is only that I have seen Mr. Starr in a new light, and I begin to esteem him somewhat."

"Well, Ryder is a good lad and deserves your approbation, but, my dear, what has brought about this change?"

"Yesterday, Papa, we met quite by accident near St. Cuthbert's and I learned Mr. Starr's secret."

The bishop leaned forward. "Secret! What secret?"

"Mr. Starr is possessed of a tender heart, though I make no doubt he would hotly deny such a charge."

"A tender heart?"

"I discovered it in the course of a conversation we had regarding his uncle."

"Ah, his uncle—a most unfortunate circumstance that the gentleman left his affairs in so peculiar a state. I have faith, however, that the present Lord Matchless will repent of his cruelty and come round to settling an income on him, though it will cost me an excellent secretary when he does. Oh dear, how I shall miss Ryder when he comes into his money."

"What I learned, Papa, was that Mr. Starr's interest is not so much in the income but in what it represents—namely, the degree of affection his uncle had for him. He wishes more than anything to know that his uncle valued him."

"That is all very well, my dear, but one cannot live on the knowledge that one was valued. One must have an income."

"Of course, Papa, and Mr. Starr is sensible enough to know that. But in addition to sense, he has feeling. That is what I had thought he lacked."

"And now you no longer think so."

"I suspect he is a gentleman whose feelings go deep."

Worried, the bishop frowned. "I expect those feelings would extend to love, would they not? That is to say, if he should fall in love with you, he would love deeply, and then I should have much to answer for to your mother in the life to come."

Aurora was on the point of laughing away her father's alarms when the face of Mr. Starr filled her imagination. She saw the stark looks he had given her on their walk to Sudsbury, felt the sensation of his touch as they danced in the meadow, recollected the laughter and vexation etched by turns on his handsome features, wondered at the myriad attributes of his smile—amusement, irony, ruefulness, gentleness, sorrow. When he had spoken of his uncle, she had been forced to repress an impulse to take his hand. What had held her back was a reluctance to pity. Nothing would be so abhorrent to him, she guessed, as the knowledge that he was pitied. More important, she did not wish him to attribute her feelings to pity; they were as far from that emotion as the moon was from Piccadilly. But if it was not pity she felt, then what was it?

Recalling the instant he had turned and walked away from her, she grew warm, conscious suddenly that she had imagined he was about to kiss her, a sensation not acknowledged until now, a sensation that was not at all disagreeable.

"My dear," said the bishop, "I believe I can permit you and Ryder to give over hating each other, but if you have any compassion for me, you will not allow him to fall in love with you. Your dear mother would never forgive me, and I should be forced to dismiss a secretary who is more than a secretary to me."

She stood and moved to the door. "Rest easy, Papa," she said on her way out. "Mr. Starr and I will no doubt quarrel again before the week is out."

"I hope so, my dear."

It gratified her to see her father smile. As she made her way along the corridor, she shook her head and laughed to think that he fretted so much about an event that was so unlikely. Should Mr. Starr fall in love with anybody, it would not be Miss Aurora Valentin. She was not at all the sort who would appeal to such a man's fancy. He had never seen her wear any colour but black; he had rarely seen her do anything but frown and disapprove. During their meetings, she had customarily treated him in the iciest manner. A gentleman who was capable of the most engaging liveliness, he would naturally be attracted to a lady of fashion, elegance and charm.

These ruminations made her stop at her chamber and forget to enter. She merely blinked at the door, not seeing it, aware only of an inexplicable sense of regret at the thought of the fashionable, elegant, charming lady who would interest Mr. Starr. If she had not been so fortunate as to recollect that he had said she was beautiful, she might well have stood in that position half the morning.

WHEN MR. STARR returned to the palace that evening, he went into the garden to consider his next move. He had scarcely begun to form a plan before the bishop called to him and welcomed him home. "For this is your home now," the old man said.

"It is a beautiful evening, Bishop. It is still light and warm. I am glad to see you are enjoying it."

"The evening is an improvement on the day. Do you know, it has been fearfully dull without you."

Ryder smiled. The bishop's simplicity was endearing, especially as it often expressed an unaffected attachment to him. "I am glad to see you, too. I must tell you what I have done. I hope you will not disapprove."

"Impossible!" the bishop declared. "If you have done it, I shall think it well done."

Mr. Starr proceeded to detail his purchases for the Horner family and his use of diocesan funds. "I shall be happy to pay the sum out of my quarter's wages, with interest, if need be," he concluded.

"Poof!" his employer replied. "You shall do no such thing. The sum will be paid from the charity box."

"You are very kind, Bishop." He would have said more, but felt himself in danger of growing sentimental. The bishop's warmth was affecting. It had taken him an entire day to pull himself out of danger from Aurora. He was not about to dash those efforts by becoming overly fond of her father.

"It is you who have been kind, Ryder. No charity is so great as that which permits a man, or in this instance, a woman, to get her own sustenance. You have done well. If circumstances had been different, you might have taken orders, you know. You would have proved a fine cleric."

"I do not think the Church would have suited me, Bishop, or rather, I should not have suited it. I may have a talent for charity, but I believe there are also certain precepts regarding chastity, for which I have no gift at all."

The bishop gazed at him. "Have you been wicked, my boy?"

"Very wicked, sir."

"That is most interesting. I have never been wicked. Nor have I ever met a very wicked gentleman, that I am aware of. You must tell me everything." On that, he led the younger man to his chambers, where, after twenty minutes of hearing exploits, borrowed principally from plays and novels, he fell into a sweet doze. The two of them sat quietly in that manner until Nussle appeared to assist the bishop to his bed, leaving Mr. Starr to think that when he did quit Sudsbury, he would assuredly miss some of its inmates.

THOUGHTS OF MR. STARR had obtruded on Aurora's consciousness so often in the course of the day that she was flustered to encounter him that evening as they both entered the parlour. Though his greeting was unexceptionable, she averted her eyes, as though she feared he might read her thoughts. Shyly, she returned his greeting, and was grateful that Nussle entered just then to ask whether they had supped. The bishop had retired, the butler reported. Would they require anything to eat? As ever, Nussle seemed to speak from a lofty height.

"I am famished," Mr. Starr said.

Aurora confessed, "I forgot supper entirely."

Mr. Starr settled comfortably into his chair and announced, "We should like the largest and tastiest supper you can supply, thank you, Nussle."

Over his nose, Nussle peered at him, replying, "I shall do what I can, sir, of course. However, I cannot answer for your supper's being either large or tasty, as cook has thrown an egg at my head in a fit of temper and does not wish to set eyes on me so long as we both shall live."

"Gracious, Nussle," Aurora said. "Why did she attack you? I have always known her to be the mildest of creatures."

"Far be it from me to presume to speak for hysterical females. Perhaps she took exception to my pointing out that the egg was overdone and not fit to feed the livestock."

Aurora's eyes met Mr. Starr's and they exchanged a smile.

"Why on earth would she take exception to such a gallant remark?" Mr. Starr asked.

"I have observed," said the butler, "that there are those who are set off by the most inconsequential things. Such thin-skinned creatures have no business endeavouring to fry an egg."

Mr. Starr said, "I fear your choice is clear, Nussle. You must either patch it up with Cook or prepare our supper with your own hands."

"I shall patch it up with her in due time," the butler stated with a slight bow. "It is a first principle with me never to patch things up too quickly. Such precipitousness might be mistaken for an apology. However, I shall contrive to have something prepared for you. I believe the kitchen maid harbours a tenderness for me and may be prevailed upon to see to your supper.'' On that, he made his way belowstairs.

''You will be pleased with me, I think,'' said Mr. Starr when they were alone.

As Aurora had already been thinking of him with pleasure for many hours, she did not dispute this assertion.

''I used the five-pound note I nearly gave to Mr. Horner yesterday to buy food and stuffs for his family.''

Aurora answered with a glowing look.

''I also appropriated a small portion of the funds the bishop authorized for roof repairs so that I might purchase gardening implements and seed for Mrs. Horner.''

''How very kind of you, Mr. Starr.''

''That is what the bishop said. I thought he might consider it somewhat high-handed of me.''

''He is too partial to you to think so. Besides, the sum ought to be paid out of the charity box. Or, at the very least, it might be considered as an advance on the payment Mr. Horner is to receive for his labours.''

''That is what I thought, too. I hoped you would be pleased.''

''I am pleased.''

''Then *I* am pleased.''

''We are both pleased,'' she said.

''It is pleasant, is it not—both of us being pleased at the same time?''

''Oh, yes, vastly pleasant.''

An awkward pause ensued. Aurora wished Nussle might return soon, for she had exhausted her store of conversation and was conscious only of Mr. Starr's presence, which seemed to rob the parlour of air.

"As you are pleased to be pleased with my small act of charity," he said, "I wonder whether I might induce you to keep the promise you made yesterday."

She raised her eyes to his. "The promise?"

"You said I might accompany you to the Samaritan Hospital."

Aurora blushed fiercely. After a pause, she said, "I have a confession to make to you. That invitation was extended out of spite."

He smiled. "I did not think you were capable of spite, Miss Valentin."

"Why not?" she retorted. "Do you think I am not subject to emotions, as other ladies are? Do you imagine that only fashionable, elegant, charming females are capable of human feeling? Do you take me for a lump of ice instead of a woman?"

Although he seemed taken aback by her fire, he replied easily, "I think you are very much a woman."

This reply again brought heat to her cheeks. "What I mean to say, Mr. Starr, is that I extended the invitation in order to punish you. I thought it would remove the smirk from your face to witness unimaginable misfortune and misery."

"Perhaps it will," he said. There was sufficient softness in his tone to encourage her to think his thoughts were not necessarily centred on ladies of elegance and fashion and charm.

Thankful that her admission had not put him off, she said, "If you wish to accompany me to the hospital, you may do so on Thursday, if my father can spare you."

"I shall see to it that he will be able to spare me." He leaned forward so that his face came close to hers.

His intentness made her put her hand to her bosom and play with the button there.

"Nothing—not storms, not floods, not wars—will keep me from visiting your hospital."

"It is only a modest building, I assure you. I hope you will not expect to see anything out of the way."

"However modest it may be, my dear Miss Valentin, a visit must prove useful. I can assure you, I intend to reap from it great profit."

NINE: A Passionate Outburst

BY THE TIME Thursday arrived, the entire town knew of the projected excursion. Many Sudsburians expressed wonder at Mr. Starr's fortitude in making a visit to the hospital, for while they themselves were generous in their contributions to it, they never went near the place if they could help it. Indeed, the principal purpose of their largesse was to excuse them from ever seeing it. They would give Miss Valentin all the money she asked for, as long as they did not have to behold any unfortunate females with their own eyes. Thus, Mr. Starr's visit was perceived as a sort of heroism, especially among the ladies of the book society. The Dickery twins echoed each other in praising his goodness and hoping he would not be made sick to his stomach by the wretched sights in store for him, while Mrs. Bludthorn whispered that his conduct was a sign of his having a tendency toward saintliness.

As they walked past the cathedral to the outskirts of the town and up the rise where the Samaritan Hospital stood, Aurora wondered if her companion would be disappointed. Although it bore the grand appellation of "hospital," the building was in fact an unprepossessing, rectangular edifice that had once served as a dairy. It had been considerably improved—the cavernous space had been broken up into commodious rooms that had been painted, furnished and made to look tidy. Nevertheless, it did not possess the imposing grey-stone aspect of a London hospital. Until now, that fact had pleased Aurora, for she had not wished it to resemble a prison, which was what most hospitals looked like to her. But glancing at Mr. Starr, and seeing his impenetrable expression, she began to think she might have erred too far on the side of simplicity. She glanced at him from time to time but was unable to read his expression.

The matron greeted them at the entrance, a clean, bright hall with a flagstone floor and no fireplace. Mrs. Hollander was an efficient, alert woman with a round pink face and a firm voice.

"I have brought a visitor," Aurora said. "I hope we do not disturb your work." She then performed an introduction.

The matron looked Mr. Starr up and down and appeared to approve. "You are welcome," she said. "We receive few visitors—too few, to my mind. They haven't the stomach for it, I expect, though if they did as you have done, and came and saw our hospital for themselves, they would see nothing to disgust, I assure you."

Aurora saw Mr. Starr smile slightly. He thanked the lady for her kindness.

"What news have you of Mercy Bates?" Aurora asked the matron. "Has there been any word from the family of Pearl Watley?"

Mrs. Hollander took up some papers from a table. "You will be happy to know that Mercy has been placed at a milliner's in Staffordshire. As to Pearl, I have located friends of hers near Stoke Poges and am confident they will be induced to take her in."

Gratified, Aurora reviewed the papers Mrs. Hollander handed her, while the matron informed Mr. Starr, "We are fortunate to be able to report, sir, that the great majority of our young women are eventually placed in honest employment or are reconciled with their families or friends."

Nodding gravely, he replied, "I should say that speaks very well for the hospital."

"Indeed it does. A considerable number of our young women are married now. Most have become useful members of society. Could their names and directions be disclosed, they would surely attest to the excellence of the work done on these premises. I am certain, once you see it for yourself, you will wish to make a donation."

Mortified, Aurora said, "Oh, Mrs. Hollander, you misunderstand. I do not bring Mr. Starr here as a prospective sponsor."

The matron wrinkled her face in puzzlement. "I thought you was a gentleman," she said to Mr. Starr.

He smiled broadly at Aurora, and with a gesture, invited her to answer.

She stammered, "He *is* a gentleman. Only he is not in a position to act as one of our benefactors."

"But I hope to be soon," Mr. Starr added, flashing a smile that was almost charming enough to enchant Mrs. Hollander.

That lady was not easily enchanted, Aurora knew, but Mr. Starr approached closer to success than any living creature had heretofore. The matron smiled back, revealing a fine set of multicoloured, crooked teeth.

"I must confess," said Mr. Starr, "that I have not been entirely useless in regard to your hospital. I did take up a collection for it at the Ladies' Book Society."

Mrs. Hollander nodded approval. "I am sure Miss Valentin and I are much obliged to you."

"*You* are, no doubt, but as to Miss Valentin, she has never said she was obliged."

Aurora blushed. Mr. Starr's manner had taken on something of its old hint of teasing. The gleam of amusement in his eyes disconcerted her. She repressed an impulse to glare at him and strove to put to use his instructions on merriment. *Remember,* she told herself, *do not permit him to put you out of countenance.* Offhandedly, she replied, "I thought it unnecessary to thank you. If you recall, you confessed that your objective had been merely to portray yourself to me in a favourable light. That effort failed dismally."

Aurora experienced satisfaction at the sight of Mr. Starr's expression. The amusement froze on his face, then faded altogether.

The effect of the remark on Mrs. Hollander was not so satisfying, however. As the matron glanced from Aurora to Mr. Starr, she began to beam at them in a heavily significant manner. Her look seemed to say that she had perceived a personal character in their relations. Once again, Aurora blushed. She hoped Mr. Starr did not find her as transparent as Mrs. Hollander did.

Leading the way, the matron took them into various wards, which were, in fact, small rooms where women were engaged in patchwork, needlework, spinning, knitting, household tasks and Bible reading. As each door opened and Mr. Starr was invited to peek inside, the young women raised their eyes, regarded him bleakly, and returned, incurious, to their work. Not one, Aurora observed, responded to his good looks. Not one betrayed interest, let alone the least suspicion of a flirting glance. Not one so much as greeted him. Aurora endeavoured to discover whether Mr. Starr was affronted by this lack of attention. She was certain he had never been treated to such a reception in his life. But it was impossible to tell what sensations he experienced; it appeared he had covered his face with a mask of impenetrability.

One thing was clear, however: he paid rapt attention to what Mrs. Hollander had to say at each stop along the tour.

"Most of our young women have never actually been forced into a life of prostitution," the matron reported. "Their families abandoned them or turned them out following the discovery that they had been seduced, and they found themselves without connections, money, recourse, shelter and friends. It would not have been surprising, in my view, if they had given up hope altogether and laid violent hands on themselves. But fortunately, they came to us instead. Here they have found a place of peace, of silent reflection and the means to an honest livelihood. Not one of them, it pains me to say, has been over the age of twenty."

Aurora watched Mr. Starr's face as he looked once at Mrs. Hollander and several times at the young women huddled in a circle, busy at their sewing. Although they presented a picture of industry and propriety, there was a resignation about them that gave the rooms an air of bleakness. These were women who truly needed Mr. Starr's lessons on merriment, Aurora thought. But perhaps such lessons would be thrown away on them; they were too sorrowful a company, too wounded and unhappy, to put such lessons to good use. Once more Aurora glanced his way. She could not help but wonder what his thoughts were. It unnerved her that he remained silent.

They toured the sick room, which was empty, the kitchen and the yard, and still Aurora could not find any sign that Mr. Starr had been impressed by what he had seen. She wished him to be moved. She wished him to reveal again that depth of feeling that had been in evidence days before and of which she knew he was capable. Yet, as the hour wore on and he responded only as politeness required, she wondered whether she had misjudged him. Perhaps he was capable of deep feeling only when his own interests were concerned. It could well be that he was indifferent to the welfare of others.

If so, she told herself, then he was not the man she had thought he was. She would not be able to esteem him. His selfishness must hold her back.

Taking leave of Mrs. Hollander at the door, they walked towards the town, not speaking for a time, following the winding path which was unadorned by trees or shrubs. At last Aurora could no longer endure his impassivity. They had nearly reached the High Street when she said, "What did you think of my hospital?"

Mr. Starr seemed not to hear.

Indignant, Aurora insisted, "Mr. Starr, I have gone to the trouble of escorting you to the hospital and of taking Mrs. Hollander from her work in order to show you about. The least you can do is to say something."

"It was, of course, most illuminating," he said sedately. "I thank you."

Aurora persisted. "That will not do. I must know what you are thinking."

She was startled to see him turn on her a pair of eyes smoky with anger. "I know what it is you expect me to say." His eyes flashed with a quiet power that made her shrink. "You expect me to make some offhand remark, something witty, frivolous and cavalier, something befitting the education and manners of a Town gentleman. You expect me to pretend that I have not seen what I have seen and that it has not affected me. You expect me to reveal the heart of stone that you have always suspected lies beneath my coat of superfine."

Astonished at his passion, Aurora could not reply.

"I am very sorry to disillusion you," he said, "but I have nothing to say. I will not cheapen or diminish what I have just witnessed by making clever observations or, indeed, any observation at all. I shall content myself with wishing you good-day, Miss Valentin," and on that, he tipped his hat and unceremoniously walked on ahead.

His figure grew smaller as he strode down the path. She watched him descend the hill, aware only that she was no longer disappointed in his lack of response. His answer struck her as wonderful, glorious, perfect. Now that he had treated her to a full-blown display of passion, unreserved and uncensored, she felt a delicious thrill. It was a wholly new experience to have been rebuked so soundly, and not at all the sort of behaviour a young lady ordinarily looked for in a handsome gentleman, but to Aurora, it was as though she had just been presented to Sir Galahad—shining armour, noble steed, Holy Grail and all.

MR. STARR FOUND NUSSLE in the kitchen, inspecting the crystal goblets. One by one, he held them up to the light, squinted critically, and buffed them with a soft cloth. Sinking into a chair, Mr. Starr said without preamble, "It is certain now, Nussle. I must leave this place."

"Yes, of course," the butler replied, setting down a polished goblet and picking up the next.

"I have offended Miss Valentin again, but this time she will not forgive me, nor will I forgive myself. I know what you will say, old friend—that you warned me of just such an eventuality as this. You will exhort me to stay and to make a new plan. And when I tell you that it is all up with me in Sudsbury, you will threaten to give up your place and accompany me on my journey. But, I tell you, Nussle, my mind is quite made up. Do not attempt to sway me."

"I hope I am not so vulgar as to do such a thing, Master Ryder."

He eyed the butler. "This is a new wrinkle. Are you ill, or have you grown weary of disputing with me?"

"No indeed, sir. I should be happy to dispute if we had the time. But a letter has come from Broome Court. I expect it is a summons."

Mr. Starr stood like a shot. "A letter! Why did you not tell me at once?"

"Far be it from me, sir, to interrupt the ramblings and rantings of my betters."

"Yes, yes, Nussle. Now stop tormenting me and hand it over."

"I do not have it in my possession, sir. The bishop has vowed to keep watch on it. Why he feels it necessary to do so, I cannot tell. I know my place too well to question the odd humours of my superiors."

Before the butler's words were out of his mouth, Mr. Starr was already on the stairs, taking them two at a time. He attained the bishop's chambers and, after an impatient scratching at the door, came in to find the old gentleman sitting at his desk, literally keeping watch on a folded paper. Mr. Starr surmised that the paper was the fateful letter from Broome Court.

"Thank heaven you have come," the bishop cried. "I was on the point of sending a servant after you." He handed Mr. Starr the letter.

Taking it, Mr. Starr paused.

"My dear boy, I know how important this is to you. Open it. Do not stand there staring at it. Open it!"

Mr. Starr tapped the unopened letter against his palm. "I have waited a very long time for this letter," he said thoughtfully. "What if it does not contain what I wish?"

The bishop went to his side and touched him bracingly on the shoulder. "Of course it contains what you wish. Why would your cousin write, if not to send good news?"

Sceptically, Mr. Starr shook his head. "With my cousin, anything is possible."

"Well, you will never know for certain unless you open it."

"Yes, of course." Slowly, he unfastened the seal and read the words scrawled over the page. He then handed it to the bishop, so that he might read the terse instruction:

Come at once.
Matchless

On reading it, the bishop hooted with glee. "It is just as I said! He wishes to see you. He intends to acknowledge you. Ah, I shall miss you when you are installed at Broome Court, but I hope I am not so selfish as to fail to wish you joy."

Mr. Starr did not share this jubilation. "It says only that he wishes me to come. He says nothing in regard to acknowledgment."

"You are too gloomy, Ryder."

"I wonder how he knew where to find me. I had written a letter to him but had not yet sent it off."

"There, that proves he wishes to acknowledge you. He went to all the trouble of finding out your direction. He would never have done so unless he wished to take you to his bosom."

"You are very kind, Bishop. I wish I were able to see it as you do."

"You must exert yourself to see it as I do, Ryder, for if I can be cheerful, surely you can. I do not look forward to losing my secretary, you know. I shall miss you dreadfully when you take up residence in Worcestershire. But you do not see me doubting and hesitating, do you?'' Here he wiped discreetly at his eye.

At this touching sentimentality, Mr. Starr smiled. ''I shall miss you, too,'' he said. ''But Worcestershire is only a morning's ride. I shall come and visit often, if you will have me.''

''Of course I will have you!'' The bishop sniffed away tears.

''I do not think so, Bishop. You see, I have quarrelled with your daughter.''

Clapping his hands, the Bishop said, ''This is excellent news.''

''You do not understand. Miss Valentin will tell you I have behaved very badly, and it will be no less than the truth. Even if you were to welcome me back for a visit, she would not.''

''Poof! Aurora never held a grudge in her life. She will soon forgive you. But that is neither here nor there. You must pack your valise and go at once to your cousin. You must not stay another instant.''

''You are right. I must lose no further time.'' He moved to the door.

''And you must take the carriage. I have already given orders to the coachman.''

Mr. Starr turned. ''You are too good, Bishop. I do not know what to say.'' He would have left then, but paused to say, ''Will you be so kind as to tell Miss Valentin for me that I am very sorry to have been obliged to leave before speaking with her? I intend to do so, however, as soon as I am able.''

''Yes, yes! I shall tell her anything you like! Only go and pack your valise before my horses wear themselves out with walking up and down in the courtyard.''

MR. STARR REQUIRED but a few minutes to fill his valise, for the past eighteen months had given him and Nussle vast experience in packing quickly. Soon he took leave of Nussle, and proceeded to the courtyard, ready to enter the carriage. The door was opened to him and the steps let down. The coachman signalled that they were ready to set off.

Before climbing aboard, Mr. Starr looked about him, reluctant to leave. As he glanced at the house, a fancy seized him to go inside, find Aurora, and explain himself to her. But the folly of such a plan was manifest. In the first place, he had no notion of where in the house she might be or if indeed she was in the house at all. In the second place, he had no idea what he would say to her if he did find her. He scarcely knew his own feelings; how could he possibly unfold them to her? In the third place, he would require several hours to give the apology he felt she deserved. And in the fourth place, there was no need to find her, for at that moment, she rounded the east wing of the house and came into view.

He went forward to meet her.

"My father told me the news. I came to wish you well." She was smiling at him with a warmth he found as magnetic as it was puzzling.

"This is very kind of you, Miss Valentin—to overlook my conduct of this afternoon."

At that allusion, she glowed. "I shall never forget it. You were amazingly forceful."

"I was rude."

"You were sincere."

He regarded her with interest. "Miss Valentin, I treated you to a scold."

Exulting, she said, "You certainly did."

"It appears you are fond of being scolded. It is not generally one of the talents for which I am renowned among the ladies, but perhaps I am not the best judge of my own accomplishments."

She moved nearer. "Mr. Starr," she said in a voice that reminded him of an arpeggio played on a harp, "you are certainly not the best judge of your own accomplishments. You scarcely know how excellent a gentleman you are."

It was clear to him now that she was far from being angry. For reasons he could not fathom, but which he meant to investigate further at the earliest opportunity, she was greatly in charity with him. "I take my leave of you reluctantly," he said, "but, regardless of what my cousin has to say to me, I shall return to continue this conversation. And perhaps, if you like, I shall treat you to another scold."

"I shall look forward to it."

Again he studied her face, and, finding no irony, finding nothing that did not bespeak the most open admiration and liking, he shook his head and gave up attempting to understand. Instead, he took her hand in both of his, brought it close to his breast to inspect it for a moment, and put her palm to his lips. It was not the farewell he wished to give her, but with the footman and coachman watching and the horses snorting and stamping their feet, he was forced to content himself with it for the moment. He entered the carriage and heard the coachman's shout and the crack of the whip. As he felt the leaders spring forward with a lurch, he tried to banish thoughts of the bishop's daughter from his head so that he might concentrate on what awaited him at Broome Court.

TEN: Truth Comes to Light

WHEN THE CARRIAGE attained the outskirts of Broome Court, Mr. Starr knocked on the roof and called to the coachman to halt. The horses had not quite drawn to a stop when he flung open the door and, before the footman could assist him, jumped to the ground. Slowly, he surveyed the farmlands, rolling in patches of green and yellow and brown on all sides of the highway. Was it his fancy, or was there a look of neglect about the houses and fields? Did he wish to believe his absence had been felt in every grain of corn and every lump of earth on the estate, or did he in truth perceive a meagreness in the crops?

Before he could answer, he found himself being greeted by a tenant.

"God save me, Master Ryder," cried the old farmer joyfully. "I never thought to lay eyes on ye again afore'n I died."

"Why, Nimms," Mr. Starr said as he shook his hand, "is it indeed you?"

Wiping a rheumy eye, Nimms mourned, "The Court han't been the same since the old Lord Matchless that was went to his grave a year ago and you was turned out. No indeed, it han't been the same."

"And is this field still yours?"

"Aye, it is, ashamed though I am to say it, for a shabby-looking business it is, I own."

"I never thought to see a field of yours look shabby, Mr. Nimms."

"I an't one to complain, as you well know, Master Ryder, but the truth air the truth and there's no use wishing it away. It's the new lord. 'E an't like the old one, nor like you neither."

"Is my cousin ill?"

A dark look crossed the farmer's leathered countenance. "Ill? I suppose there's them as might say he was, and them as might say he warn't."

"What do *you* say, Mr. Nimms?"

"I say if you be meaning to visit the Great House, there's awaiting you a sight you never thought to see. I say no mor'n that, lest you think it be idle gossip I be putting in yer ear." On that, he called to another tenant, who had just turned with his mule onto the road.

Like Nimms, the tenant started upon recognizing Mr. Starr and greeted him, saying, "Master Ryder, sir, ye'r a sight for eyes that air sore with seeing a world gone to the divvil."

For a considerable time, the two farmers bemoaned the decline of the once-great Broome Court and then Mr. Starr remounted the carriage and drove off. What the farmers had said, and even more what they had hinted at, gave the impression that his cousin was in a grave condition. He concluded that illness was the reason Frederick had sent for him—he needed help managing the estate. If that was the case, he did not know how he ought to respond. It would give him the greatest pleasure to live once again at the Court. On the other hand, it would be a blow to his pride to return as steward.

One thing was certain: if his services were required, he would not allow them to go uncompensated. Nothing must be left to chance or to mere verbal understanding this time.

A lawyer must draw up a contract so that Ryder might know
precisely where he stood and precisely what he might expect. There would be no reliance on promises and protes-
tations of regard. He would not make the mistake with the
son that he had made with the father.

As the countryside between the Bath Road and the London Road was not abundant in stately houses, coming upon
Broome Court was always a shock for any traveller. It was
not only one of the finest edifices along the southeast route
towards the Cotswolds, it was one of the grandest in
Worcestershire. The first Matchless had served the kingdom as Lord Keeper in the days of the peace-loving, schol-
arly Henry VII, and his monument in the local church bore
the Great Seal of England. He had begun the building of
Broome Court, which was not completed until the sixth
Lord Matchless employed Robert Adam in 1752. Around
the old buildings, Adam had constructed a Palladian house
with a two-armed open staircase at the entrance and a garden portico of fluted Doric columns in the rear. The splen-
dour of the house and its park had ever since been a
watchword throughout the county, but as the carriage drew
up, and Mr. Starr gazed from the window, he saw signs of
dereliction. He was glad his uncle was not alive to see it.

As soon as he alighted from the carriage, he found that he
had been followed by Mr. Nimms, the other farmer, and a
host of tenants who had joined them along the way. They
were a clamorous band, especially the women among them,
who, observing Mr. Starr step down to the gravel walk,
rained on him questions concerning his health, happiness
and marital status. Several young ladies brought forth bas-
kets containing the fruits of early summer—lettuce, cold-
frame cucumbers and strawberries—and offered him gifts
of welcome. He would have taken all their hands and kissed

them had not the housekeeper issued forth and shooed them away as though they were so many chickens.

Mrs. Verbost cocked her grey head and looked the gentleman up and down. "So you've come home, have you, Master Ryder? It's high time you woke to your senses. I vow, I don't know what you were thinking of to go off and leave us all. For shame."

"I didn't leave you, dear Mrs. Verbost. I was dismissed." He bowed over her hand with silky gallantry, then brought it ostentatiously to his lips.

Red and white by turns, the housekeeper evaded the eyes of the crowd, which stared at her with glee or envy, depending on whether they were male or female, and ordered, "You must come inside. His lordship will be wishing to see you. It's best not to keep him waiting."

She then shouted at his admirers to go away so that Mr. Starr might get on with his business, as they ought to be doing themselves, if only they had the sense of peahens.

When Mr. Starr entered the hall, he noticed at once that, like everything else he had observed on the estate, the interior of the house had deteriorated. The once-gorgeous blue-painted ceiling was peeling. On the grand stairway, the carpet was worn and the wood railings had lost their ornaments. The white, sculpted caryatides in the gallery were sadly chipped, while the alcoves, which had once been filled with antique figures against a background of grisaille sketches, were empty, giving rise to the suspicion that the sculpture had been sold off. There pervaded throughout an atmosphere of gloom. Rooms he remembered as being bright and tidy, filled with fresh flowers and the scent of lavender, now seemed oppressive, stale and dark. The Samaritan Hospital was a paragon of jollity by comparison.

While Mrs. Verbost went to announce his arrival to his lordship, Mr. Starr reviewed the family portraits, pausing long and thoughtfully before the face of his uncle. The man's English nose and square jaw struck him as even finer than he had recalled. In his eyes was an expression of kindness. One could not glimpse such a countenance without seeing a man of honour. Unable to look anymore, Mr. Starr turned away.

Mrs. Verbost came in, not to fetch him as he had expected, but to announce, in considerable consternation, that Lord Matchless was not in a humour to receive visitors.

"When does he wish to see me?" Mr. Starr enquired.

"He cannot say." She bit her lip in apology.

"Perhaps you are mistaken, Mrs. Verbost. You see, in his note, my cousin said I was to come immediately. His summons appeared urgent."

The housekeeper made an effort at a smile. "Never you mind about urgent. It is too late for visiting today. Tomorrow will be better. Now, you must rest and take some refreshment. Let me show you to your old room. I shall make you a dinner of haricot of lamb and pudding."

Mr. Starr frowned. His cousin's behaviour was puzzling. He wondered if Frederick had had second thoughts about meeting with him. It would not surprise him, for his cousin was a capricious fellow.

There and then, Mr. Starr made a decision: he would not be refused. If Frederick was still denied to him at the end of a reasonable time, he would be obliged to take action. What that action was, he would have been hard-pressed to say, but now that he had returned to Broome Court, he did not intend to be turned out of it again so easily.

During the following days, he engaged himself in calling on the tenants. He visited the stables and found his old horse, Gulliver. It galled him to find that his cousin had had the stallion gelded—that instead of putting to stud one of the finest specimens of horseflesh ever to trot on English soil, he had ended the line entirely. Mr. Starr could not ignore the supposition that the horse's fate had been intended to punish its owner.

When he was not acquainting himself with the affairs of the estate, Mr. Starr busied himself with nodding to the young ladies who happened by on various pretexts and with tasting the delicacies Mrs. Verbost prepared for him, rhapsodizing over her venison pie, her collier's roast, her rabbit cup, kissing her cheek and flirting with her mercilessly. The woman wept with pleasure to have Master Ryder home again where he belonged and where, she informed him roundly, he never should have left to begin with.

"Confess it, Mrs. Verbost," he teased one afternoon over tea in what once had been a sumptuous green salon, "it is not Master Ryder you have missed but Mr. Nussle."

The woman turned crimson. "I'm sure I don't know what you mean, sir. I'm sure I don't give the man a thought, nor does he give one to me, I'm sure."

"It would be an excellent thing to have Nussle here again. He would put the place to rights in the blinking of an eye."

"Has he ever spoken of me?" the housekeeper enquired with an attempt at unconcern.

"Mr. Nussle has never spoken of you," he said.

Her face fell.

"Except with the utmost respect and courtesy."

"Oh!"

He smiled. "He does not get on with the cook at the bishop's palace, I fear. She throws eggs at his head."

"Ah, the poor man. If he were to come back home, I should see that he was treated as he deserves."

"He will never come back, my good Mrs. Verbost, if my cousin does not send for me soon. It has been four days now and still he has refused to admit me to his sanctum."

Dejected, the housekeeper shook her head. "Shall I go and ask him again if he will receive you?"

He set aside his cup and plate and rose from his chair. "No, my dear lady. It is my turn now. I shall go, and he will speak to me, whether he is in a receiving humour or not."

Wringing her hands, she cried, "Oh, do not go in to him unannounced. He is not himself. Some harm will come of it."

He patted her cheek, kissed it with a smack, and marched off to the library, from which his cousin had not stirred, so far as he knew, since the day he had quitted Broome Court.

When his knocking received no answer, he tried the knob and found it locked. For some time, he called to his cousin. When it was clear that the man had no intention of replying, Mr. Starr raised one neatly booted foot and kicked the door soundly. It gave way, to reveal Frederick Matchless, his head in his hands on his father's writing desk. Apparently, he had heard neither the noise of the door being kicked open nor the approach of his cousin. For an instant, Mr. Starr wondered if the man was dead.

As he entered, he saw that the library was a shambles. It appeared it had not been dusted since his uncle's funeral. Books lay everywhere, their pages open, their bindings torn. Traces of half-eaten suppers were scattered over chairs. The single narrow casement was covered with a cloth, and the room seemed to swallow every breath of air.

Then Mr. Starr saw the empty bottle and overturned glass on the floor at Frederick's feet. Leaning over him, pushing him by the shoulders to an upright position, he said, "So, Freddy, this is why you have refused to see me. You have had a more important appointment to keep, with your brandy."

Unable to sit straight, Frederick slumped back against the chair. His head rolled, as did his eyes. At last they came to rest on Mr. Starr, who waited for his cousin to recognize him.

When he did, his face contorted. "Get out," he rasped.

"May I remind you, Freddy, that you sent for me?"

"Do not call me that! I despise you. With all my heart, I despise you."

"Yes, yes, cousin, you have already said that. I dare say if you persist in repeating yourself, there are those who will think you bosky. Now, to the heart of the matter. Why did you send for me?"

"The sight of you makes me sick!"

"I see. And do you often send for those who put you in such an unpleasant state? How very odd. I myself prefer to see those who delight me. Permit me to say, however, that you are far from being the prettiest sight I have ever beheld—or smelt."

Frederick retched. "Go away."

"No, dear Freddy. I believe I shall sit right here until you tell me precisely why I have been sent for." On that, he planted himself in a chair and made himself entirely comfortable.

His lordship pulled himself to his feet, paused to let a wave of nausea pass, and took a step towards his cousin, waving an accusing finger in his direction. "I have received letters. They come from everywhere. They say you have behaved most despicably."

Mr. Starr confirmed this with a nod. "Oh, yes, most despicably, I assure you. I was quite terrified, you know, that the truth would one day come to light and you would be in a frightful pet. But now that it has come to pass, I see it is not so awful as I dreaded, and I freely confess it all."

White with anger, Frederick shouted, "You are deliberately destroying the Matchless name."

"I expect I am, but you may easily persuade me to cease and desist. All you need do is give me what was promised, and I shall hereafter comport myself like a saint."

Closing his eyes, Frederick put a hand to his forehead and steadied himself. "Nothing was promised you."

Unsmiling, Mr. Starr replied, "You know that is a lie."

"If it is a lie, then produce the evidence! Produce the clause in my father's will that proves it." He laughed wildly. "You cannot do that, can you?"

Mr. Starr stood and came close to his cousin. Because the man swayed dangerously, he steadied him with a hand on his shoulder. "Tell me, Freddy, I have heard it said that there is such a will, or at least a codicil, and that you might produce it if you would. Is it so? Do you hate me so much, are you so jealous of your father's supposed love for me, that you have destroyed the will? Have you, Freddy?"

Matchless cringed, staring at Mr. Starr.

"Your eyes, Cousin, are the eyes of a guilty man. Tell me, what are you afraid of?"

On that, Lord Matchless raised his hand and hit Mr. Starr with all his force. Though that force was not very great, owing to his drunkenness and poor health, he wore a ring that brought blood to Mr. Starr's cheek.

Mr. Starr's initial instinct was to retaliate, but he restrained himself, for it went against the grain with him to strike a man one could fell with a feather. More important, he knew his uncle would have wished him to behave like a gentleman. "You always did have a vile temper, Freddy," he said. "But for my uncle's sake, I shall offer you my hand." The gesture of peace cost him considerable effort, for he held his cousin in no more esteem than a worm.

The outstretched hand was more than Frederick could endure. He let out a howl and attacked Mr. Starr with such fury that both of them were flung against the wall, knocking over a nearby table and all its contents. It was not difficult for Mr. Starr to deflect Frederick's onslaught, for even if his lordship had not been in his cups, he was too weak and ungainly to do much harm. But while Ryder defended himself, he could not bring himself to inflict any blows in retaliation.

This forbearance inflamed Frederick to the point of frenzy. He threw himself upon his cousin, flailing at him so wildly that he fell to the carpet. Mr. Starr held his cousin's arms, pinning him to the floor, and attempted to calm him, but the man would not be calmed. He shouted incoherent threats in which only the words *deserve killing* could be distinguished.

The servants rushed in, led by Mrs. Verbost. Mr. Starr rose, lifting Frederick with him, and sent him reeling into the housekeeper's ample arms. He stood a moment, watching Frederick thrash and rant. It was a pitiful sight. His uncle would have been anguished to see his son so reduced. But it was vain, he knew, to think of such things now, for the truth was he could accomplish nothing here. Any hopes the summons to Broome Court had raised had now effectively been dashed by Frederick's consuming rancour.

Less than fifteen minutes later, Mr. Starr climbed aboard the bishop's carriage and was on his way back to Sudsbury. He could not wait to leave that place, which held pleasant memories for him no longer. The only question was, what lay ahead? He was worse off now than ever. There was no hope of regaining his inheritance and there never would be. He must now set about making his way in the world in earnest.

But what was he to do? It was impossible to continue his pose as secretary to the bishop. That had done for an interval, while he had a scheme in view, but it would not do for a lifetime. He must look to establish some dignity, some position in the world, if not for his own sake, then for Aurora's. If he wished her to think of him as more than an upper servant in her father's household, he must make something of himself. Otherwise he would never be worthy of her regard. He would not be able to present himself to her in the character of a friend, and certainly not as a lover.

AURORA COULD NOT recollect when she had been so absent-minded. She would lay down *The Vicar of Wakefield* to fetch a bit of seed for the canary. She would forget what errand she had gone on and return empty-handed. Sitting again, she would look to continue her reading and pick up a volume of Cowper's poems. Regardless of what she read, she absorbed not a word. It was as though an object lurked just outside her range of vision, and no matter how studiously she concentrated, she could not locate it. All she knew was that when her father lamented Mr. Starr's absence, she was aware of something stopping her throat.

A dozen or more times a day, she passed his bedchamber. She paused outside, half expecting that he would emerge, smile, tease her, arrest her with his grey eyes and take her breath away with the force of his presence. After three days of repeating this habit, it occurred to her that she wished him home—by which she meant the bishop's palace. The other place he called home, Broome Court, had kept him far too long.

That he was absent so many days did not bode well, she thought. His cousin wished to keep him there and purposely delayed his return. Perhaps he would not return for weeks or even months—perhaps never. The possibility alarmed her. She went so far as to ask her father whether he thought Mr. Starr would simply send for his things and not return to the palace at all. The bishop replied in horror, "He must return. I will not hear of his not returning."

Of course he would return, Aurora assured herself. For one thing, he had promised he would. She recalled the tenderness with which he had held her hand to his breast. She felt his kiss on her palm. Those recollections succeeded in suffusing her neck with heat. Oh, he must return, she told herself. Their situation was too full of questions, too ripe, for him not to.

She caught herself sighing and mooning and could not help smiling. If she had been a simpering London miss, she could not have seemed more daft. One would think she was in love.

She laughed at the very idea, then shivered. *In love.* The notion was suddenly not amusing. It was too close to the truth to be amusing. All she had to do was summon the image of his face, the passion in his voice as he'd upbraided her, the power of his expression as he'd danced with her in the meadow, and she knew it was no jest.

How was it possible that she could perform such a turnabout? How was it possible that she could esteem the man she had so lately despised, and not merely esteem him, but love him? The answer, she acknowledged, was that he had been right in his early estimation of her: the reason she had disliked him so intensely was that she liked him, liked him far too well. His audacity, his banter, his oozing charm, his challenging eyes, his insufferable smile, his insouciance were magnetic. They had put her off because she had felt drawn to them. She had known herself to be in danger, and with good reason.

She roamed the corridors, her thoughts in Worcestershire, her fancies in the future. Her feet, however, remained in the palace and, accordingly, made their way to the parlour, where her father waited for her to join him at supper.

When Nussle brought in the cold roasted fowl and saffron bread, the Bishop sighed and enquired, "Nussle, has there been any word from Broome Court? I should think there would be some word after all this time."

"It has scarcely been four days," the butler replied.

"Is it really only four days? I felt sure it was longer. It seems so much longer. Oh, dear, I cannot recall when I have felt so low—not since Mrs. Valentin departed this vale of tears. The palace is fearfully dull of late, isn't it, Nussle?"

Nussle made certain that Aurora had everything she required and then bowed. "Far be it from me, Bishop," he said, "to remark upon the gloom and tediousness of a house and its inmates. You will, however, pardon my observing that no house can compare to the comfort and joy of Broome Court."

On that, he excused himself, leaving Aurora with the apprehension that Mr. Starr would find Broome Court so accommodating, so lively and welcoming, that he would forget her and her father and Sudsbury altogether. She was contemplating this catastrophe and was very near tears when Nussle returned, bringing her a letter, which had been brought by messenger. She took it from him eagerly, thinking it was from Mr. Starr. But upon opening it, she found it to have been dated at Nardingham, a name that sounded familiar but that she could not place at first.

"Is it from Ryder?" the bishop asked hopefully.

"I am afraid it is not," Aurora replied. Nussle bowed himself out once more, while the Bishop sighed mournfully and comforted himself with a bite of pudding. Aurora, meanwhile, read as follows:

My dear Miss Valentin,
You will, I hope, pardon my delay in replying to your letter of enquiry in regard to the character of Mr. Ry-

der Starr. As the only lawyer in the town, I am, as you might imagine, quite overwhelmed with correspondence. In this case, however, I was prevented from writing immediately by the necessity of travelling. I have lately visited the villages of Clodham, Upchalk and Littledell, the inhabitants of which speak of Mr. Starr as the residents of Nardingham do—as a charlatan, a swindler and a thief. That is to say, the landholders and the other gentlemen speak of him so. The ladies, I regret to say, insist upon defending him, despite the evidence. Judging by your letter, however, I have every confidence that you are one female who has not been taken in by his chicanery. Naturally, you will wish to know the particulars of these charges, and they are these: to wit, that Mr. Starr ingratiated himself with the ladies of the aforementioned towns, as well as Nardingham, by dint of flirtation and hints and implied promises; that having won their confidence, he then divided them from their money and their sense by persuading them to donate to a charity; that having driven the ladies distracted, he was approached by the gentlemen and asked discreetly to leave, that the price of his leaving was an extortionate sum of money and a letter of character. This, then, is my conclusion and the conclusion of the other townspeople with whom I have consulted: that Mr. Ryder Starr's purpose in coming into our midst was purely and simply to be bribed to leave, and that he never had any interest whatsoever in the Samaritan Hospital....

Aurora read no further. Pressing her hand against her lips, she contrived to stifle a cry. Suddenly, she stood, startling her father. The letter fell from her lap as she ran from the room.

"What is it, my dear?" the bishop called after her. But it was too late. She was gone. Easing out of his chair, he went to retrieve the fallen letter. As he picked it up, he happened to see the name *Ryder Starr*. His curiosity was piqued, and this presented him with a moral dilemma. Was he to read a letter addressed to his daughter, a letter that had obviously overset her and that pertained to a young gentleman he regarded almost as a son—a young gentleman, moreover, who might be in difficulty and require his assistance? Or was he to fold the letter again, put it away, and return it to Aurora without another thought of prying into her private matters? Tapping the letter against his cheek, the bishop wondered what his wife would have instructed him to do.

ELEVEN: In Which Nothing Much Happens

IN HER SITTING-ROOM, Aurora paced, sat, stood and paced again. She could make no sense of the letter's contents, for she was by turns hot and freezing, restless and deadly calm. According to the letter from Nardingham, Mr. Starr, for whom she had so lately shed tears of love, was a fraud and a swindler. His activities since arriving in Sudsbury were apparently of a piece with what he had perpetrated in every other town he had visited. She recalled what Nussle had let slip in regard to Mr. Starr's habit of making his way in the world by lying and trickery. That inadvertent remark had caused her to write to Mr. Aycock. And now she had had her answer.

She paused in her pacing. What, she wondered, did the Samaritan Hospital have to do with Mr. Starr? As far as she knew, the gentleman had never heard of it before arriving in Sudsbury. The question gripped her and would not let her go. No doubt there was some mischief afoot, and she must not permit the hospital to be harmed by it.

Then a thought occurred to her, a thought so appalling, so uncharacteristic, so wicked that she gasped. She sank onto the sofa, amazed at her own audacity. No, no, she repeated to herself. She must not submit to such an impulse. He would never forgive her if he discovered it. She would never forgive herself.

Her eyes stung, but they soon dried as the lawyer's words came home to her again. He had praised her for being too strong and sensible to be taken in by Mr. Starr's wiles. That praise reproached her now, for in truth, she was more foolish than the entire female population of four English villages; she not only had been taken in by the man, she loved him beyond speech, beyond reason, beyond principle.

Again the shocking notion took hold of her, and again she scolded herself for thinking vile thoughts. It was out of the question, she told herself, speaking aloud to the canary, who cocked his head, as though he found her words fascinating. "The bishop's daughter cannot stoop to subterfuge," she told the bird. "If she does, she is no better than Mr. Starr. Have I not declared that the first wish of my heart is to refrain from interfering? Is this not interference of the worst kind?"

She threw herself onto the sofa in dejection as the questions raged in her head. It was true she did not wish to interfere, but she was responsible for the welfare of the Samaritan Hospital, which was somehow concerned in Mr. Starr's affairs. As its founder, sponsor and principal, was she not obligated to investigate further? Did she not have a duty to protect the hospital by any and every means?

Grimly, she went to the door. Taking a breath for courage, she turned the handle and went out. As she walked along the narrow, ancient corridor, she felt like a malefactor about to meet the hangman. At the door to Mr. Starr's chamber, she stopped to search her ring of keys. When she had located the proper one, she paused to send up a prayer for pardon. Then she let herself in.

It was a cosy chamber, bright with blue-flowered paper and warm mahogany. Because the curtains were only partly drawn, a rectangle of late-afternoon light permitted her to see. Carefully, as though the floor were checkered with nails, she moved about the room, stopping to inspect an ivory cravat dangling from an ornament on the looking-glass. She picked up a shaving razor and then a fine beaver hat that sat atop the highboy.

On the bed lay a book. She leaned down to see its title. It was *Persuasion*. Judging by the paper tucked into the pages, Mr. Starr was actually reading the novel. Her head ached, her throat was raw. She sat down wearily on the bed and took up the book. It opened to a conversation in which the heroine argued forcefully that women were capable of loving as steadfastly as men. The paper that marked the place was thick and fine, and because she had already invaded Mr. Starr's sanctum, she thought it could not be very much more evil to open the sheet and see what it contained. She read the following:

My Dear Cousin Matchless,

It has been a considerable time since you banished me from Broome Court, and in that time you have neither answered my letters nor given any indication of having received them. You are aware that my unjust treatment at your hands would pain your father, who expressed, in your hearing as well as mine and that of many witnesses, a wish to see us equally well provided for so that we might live as brothers. You cannot in conscience continue to ignore his wishes. In honour of his memory, I propose to you that we set aside past differences and come to a settlement. You may write to me at the palace of the Bishop of Sudsbury.

I am yours, etc.

The letter contained no signature, only an insignia: a star listing languidly to the east.

Aurora did not move for some time. Carefully, she replaced the letter in the book, thinking that she had received precisely what she deserved—the very information that

would most torment her. Mr. Starr was her mysterious benefactor, the gentleman who had occupied her dreams and
her thoughts for many months now, the one she had wished
so ardently to meet and find handsome, charming, educated and as passionate as herself. It just proved, she
thought, how very disagreeable it could be to have one's
fondest dreams come true. To add to her mortification, she
found that her cheeks were wet. She had not even known she
was weeping.

Resolutely, she forced herself to think. And think she did,
for several intense moments, but all this mighty effort
yielded was the conclusion that she was hopelessly attached
to a man who was a liar and a trickster.

Her attention was caught suddenly by the sound of the
door creaking. It opened wide, and before she could wish
that she might sink into the earth, Mr. Starr entered.

He swung the door shut. She could see he was preoccupied with some trouble. It seemed to Aurora that he was
short of breath. Perhaps, she thought, the constraints of his
attire choked him, for he unbuttoned his coat irritably, removed it and tossed it onto a chair. His pale green waistcoat met the same fate. With an impatient tug, he loosened
his cravat and, after opening his shirt, inhaled deeply. Having never seen a gentleman in a state of semi-undress, Aurora experienced a flush of confusion. He took another
breath and, turning, saw her. She steeled herself.

For what seemed an eternity, he looked at her. Gradually, his expression softened. He came to her and sat next to
her on the bed. Taking her hands, he glanced at them, then
at her face. It seemed as if he could not look hard enough.
"Thank you for coming," he said and drew her to him.

Aurora found that though he kissed her over and over,
covering her face and her hair and her ears with his lips, she
could not find the strength to push him away, rise in indig-

ation and denounce him as she ought. Instead, she let her head drift back so that he might kiss her neck and glide his hands along her arms and back. Her eyes closed as she allowed herself to be carried along by his whisperings, which were scarcely distinct but which nonetheless conveyed fervour, longing, and, much to her amazement, gratitude.

All at once, she felt his lips pressed to hers. He held her so close that she felt consumed. There was desperation in the strength of his arms round her. She felt herself engulfed by a sensation that was new and familiar at the same time—passion—and it equalled his own. As she allowed it to burst its confines, she felt his surprise, his thankfulness, his increased ardour. For the first time in her life, she was losing herself, being propelled by a current she could not combat, because she did not wish to.

Abruptly, he held her away. Her eyes opened. He stood, and as he raked his hand through his hair, he fixed her with a serious gaze. She thought he had never looked more manly. He lifted a chair and brought it to the bedside, placing it just in front of her. "You will keep this here until I have finished speaking," he said.

His words were incomprehensible. Indeed, she had understood nothing since reading the letter from Narlingham. She must bestir herself now to clear her head and regain her composure.

"That chair will be your protection until I have said what I have to say. Is that understood?"

When she could do no more than stare at him, wide-eyed, he explained, "Aurora, have you any notion how difficult it is for me to keep my distance?"

She shook her head.

"Suffice it to say, it is the very devil. But I must not come near you, at least not until I have told you everything. Do you understand?"

She nodded, knowing in her soul that she understood nothing.

"My reason for coming to Sudsbury was to kick up a scandal. It is my practice to raise a to-do wherever I go, so that the townspeople will write to my cousin and inform him of my dastardly conduct. He would be forced to recognize me and my claims, I reasoned, merely to keep me out of mischief. I had been successful in four villages before arriving at the palace and had every hope that I would induce the bishop to cry out against me and drive my cousin to do what was right. However, I experienced a slight difficulty when I discovered your connection to the Samaritan Hospital, because, you see, it was my solicitation of funds for that charity that allowed me to ingratiate myself with the townspeople, especially the ladies. I was never more amazed than when I learned that the hospital was located here and that you were its sponsor. It was the damnedest coincidence."

Aurora had some difficulty in following this tale, but she heard one piece of it with absolute lucidity: his deception had not been calculated to harm anybody. When all was said and done, he had done no actual wrong as far as she could see, which, she acknowledged to herself, was not very far at the moment, given the distraction caused by Mr. Starr's state of dishabille. But though she could not see perfectly, she could feel, and she felt she could not quite share Mr. Starr's view of the circumstances, for she had never believed in coincidence. She had been used to calling it by another name: Providence.

"It seemed I would be obliged to quit Sudsbury," he said, "but, luckily or unluckily, I invented another scheme, to wit, I would make you fall in love with me. Aurora, do you hear what I am saying? I deliberately schemed to win your affections."

She nodded. She could not find the words to tell him how very successful his scheme had turned out.

"You look very odd," he said and began to approach, but stopped himself. "It is no wonder. I dare say you did not know until now that so much depravity existed in the entire world as is here collected in one man. Unfortunately, I have not done yet. You see, though you did not know it, you were revenged in the end. My scheming against you accomplished one thing—I fell in love with you. There you have it, and I hope it gives you much satisfaction to know that I got what I never bargained for."

"Oh, yes, it is very satisfying."

"I am obliged to tell you that Nussle knew of the plan, but he never approved. Regardless of what you may think of me, you must not condemn him."

"You love me," she exulted.

"Stay behind the chair, if you please."

His passion as he said it made her smile. He looked very well without his coat, she thought.

"It is no matter whether I love you," he went on. "I cannot offer for you. I have nothing. My cousin has refused to recognize me and my claims. There is no hope for it. I must leave Sudsbury and find a means of keeping myself, something that does not depend on the Samaritan Hospital."

"I must thank you for the kind donations you sent."

"You must not thank me. Had I pocketed the money, I should have been found out and put in prison. It was not generosity that prompted me, merely a desire to save my skin."

"Nevertheless, you were the instrument by which I was able to install a bake oven to teach the making of gateau and tarts. You have been useful, whatever your motive, and so I thank you."

As though it were a feather, he removed the chair and sat down near her, cupping her cheeks tenderly with his hands. "I am the one who must give thanks. When I entered this chamber, I was like a man going to the gallows. Wherever I looked, I saw bleakness. I told myself there was no sense, no comfort, no real affection in this world. And all at once there you were. I shall never forget it. I looked up and saw your face and knew I was wrong."

"And then you kissed me."

"Ah, you remember that, do you?"

"I have a vague recollection of it, yes."

"Perhaps I ought to refresh your memory." So saying, he kissed her eyes. "I believe this is how it was done," he said, and lightly kissed her lips. Aurora wondered how it was that she could feel so miserable one moment and so blessed the next. It must be, she concluded, that there was something enchanted in Mr. Starr's kisses, or in the glow of his eyes, or in the manner in which he unbuttoned her collar and admired what he uncovered.

But enchantment aside, now that he had made his confession, she must make hers. By this time, he had loosed her collar even more and nestled his mouth against her skin. Hence, it required rather a monumental effort to put two coherent words together, let alone a full confession. But as he had composed himself long enough to explain himself to her, surely she could do as much for him.

Easing herself away, she sought out the chair. She placed it in front of him and said breathlessly, "I, too, must speak."

He took advantage of the fact that she stood before him in full view. She felt as if she stood there in her shift.

"If you must explain," he said, "do so quickly, my love. I should not like to lose any time in returning to our original line of conversation."

She cleared her throat. "No doubt you are wondering what brought me here at this hour."

He reached over the chair and grasped her hand. "I know what brought you here. And I do not know when I have received a sweeter surprise."

"Oh, Ryder, you will be disappointed. It was only a letter that brought me here. But I am very glad it did, very glad. The important thing, I think, is that I was here when you came in and you were glad to see me."

"What letter?"

"A letter from Nardingham, from a lawyer there."

He withdrew his hand.

"I wrote to him shortly after you arrived at the palace. I wished to know more of your character. At the time, I was suspicious of your conduct, as you no doubt guessed. I was determined to hunt up information to your detriment. The letter was Mr. Aycock's reply."

His old smile flickered across his lips. She noticed that it was a hard smile.

"No doubt he related everything he knew to my detriment, which was a great deal," he said.

"Yes, no, that is to say, he related everything you have just told me. But it does not matter, for you have told me everything yourself, and I believe you."

His eyes narrowed. "Did you also write to my cousin?" There was an edge to his voice. "Is that how he knew where to find me?"

Colouring, Aurora said, "Yes, I wrote to your cousin. But that was before I knew you, knew what you were truly capable of."

He gave her a cynical smile.

She guessed the hundred bitter sensations that he was experiencing and, pushing aside the chair, went to stand before him. Gently, she put her hands to his dark hair, then brought his head to the warmth of her breast and held him close.

He did not move. She sensed his resistance and stroked his hair. As his cheek rested against her, she sensed he would not long be able to withstand her touch. He must feel the throb of her pulse, the rise and fall of her bosom. She had just summoned the courage to tell him that she loved him when a rude banging at the door made her start.

Turning around, she saw her father enter. He waved a paper in the air and beckoned to a man who peeked inside.

"Arrest that villain!" the bishop commanded. He pointed to Mr. Starr.

"No!" Aurora cried out.

"Yes," the bishop contradicted, pushing forward the man who had accompanied him.

Folding his arms, Mr. Starr shook his head, laughed and declared, "This is the devil of a time for one's sins to come home to roost."

"What is the charge?" the constable whispered loudly to the bishop.

"You know very well what the charge is," the old man said. He wiped away a tear and sniffled.

"Do I?" the constable mused. "Well, then I suppose I have forgot."

"You saw him with your own eyes," the bishop cried. "He was discovered with my daughter, locked in fond embrace."

The constable leaned forward to confide, "I do not think that is unlawful, sir."

"Father," Aurora said with quiet dignity, "I can understand your forming certain conclusions based upon what you witnessed when you entered, but I assure you, you have misunderstood."

The bishop turned to the constable with impatience. "What are you waiting for? Arrest him."

The constable cleared his throat. "I am only too happy to oblige, sir, but I must have cause. This is a civilized country and we cannot arrest anybody and everybody because we dislike them, though it would be very agreeable, I'm sure, if we could."

Mr. Starr inhaled and rose. Moving to the casement, he looked out at a distant sprawling chestnut tree, as though the debate in progress did not concern him.

"Mr. Starr has done nothing," Aurora said.

"He has proved himself a scoundrel and a thief!" the bishop said. "I have the proof of it." He waved the letter from Nardingham under her nose.

"Papa, you have read my letter," she exclaimed. "That was very wrong of you."

"I cannot believe my ears. You, too, have read this letter, and still you defend him!"

"What has he done to anger you so, Papa?"

"He has imposed upon me in the most heartless manner, that is what he has done. He has induced me to love him, merely in order to profit by it. He has no regard for me at all."

"Do not, I beg you, be deceived by appearances."

"It has all been falsehood, from beginning to end. Oh, if his Fontinella could see what he has come to now!"

At this unfortunate allusion, Aurora blushed mightily.

Mr. Starr turned from the window to say, "There is no Fontinella, Bishop. That was falsehood, too, as Miss Valentin knows full well."

"Angels in Heaven, you knew it, Aurora! Even Fontinella was a hoax. He has not scrupled to use the dead and departed to further his schemes. It has all been fraud, and I shall see him in jail for it."

Earnestly, Aurora pleaded, "Perhaps he has not been entirely honest, but he has broken no law."

"Oh, but he has. He has. Did he not use two pounds six-pence to purchase gardening implements and seed for Mrs. Horner? And did he not do this without my express authorization?"

"Papa! You know why Mr. Starr used the money as he did. You know what he meant by it. You must not bear him such ill will as to fabricate a pretext for arresting him."

With profound sorrow, the bishop said, "He has broken my heart, Aurora. He will break yours as well. That is what men of his sort do, they break the hearts of those who come to love them."

On this, Mr. Starr turned round and faced the father, the daughter and the minion of the law.

"Well, what have you to say for yourself, sir?" the bishop demanded.

Mr. Starr walked to where he had flung his clothes. Un-hurriedly, he put them on, and after adjusting his coat neatly and brushing the lapel, said, "I am at your service, Constable. Whenever you are at leisure, you may escort me to my new lodgings."

"Do not despair, Ryder," Aurora urged. "I shall talk to my father. All will be well."

He tilted his head slightly in order to study her. "My compliments," he said with a nod of respect. "You have done well. I would not have thought it, but you have schemed more successfully than I could ever boast."

She blinked. "I do not understand."

"Why, this trap you have set—meeting me here in my chamber so that I would have no opportunity, and cer-tainly no desire, to escape, then keeping me so well enter-tained until your father could arrive with the constable. It was brilliantly conceived, brilliantly executed."

"You think I came here to trap you?"

"I may have greater experience in the falsehood line, my dear Miss Valentin, but you are possessed of a greater natural gift." With a mock bow and flourish, he turned to the constable. "Now, my good man, would you do me the honour of taking me to jail as quickly as possible? I find the air in here suffocating."

TWELVE: Prisoner

AURORA LOOKED at her father, but her unspoken plea was useless. His eyes lighted everywhere but on her.

"Papa," she implored, "I believe Mr. Starr holds you in great affection and esteem, and when you have had time to consider, you will see that I am right. You will forgive him."

"I think not," said the bishop, wagging his head mournfully. "Even if I might come to forgive him for what he has done to me, I could not forgive his betrayal of you."

"How do you imagine he has betrayed me?"

"He has made you fall in love with him. Oh, do not attempt to deny it. I know your heart, Aurora. I can see you love him."

"I do not deny it."

"There, you see! Your mother will skin me alive."

"But Mama is dead."

Darkly, he said, "She will find a way."

Seeing that her father was not likely at the moment to be receptive to rational argument, she said, "I expect it would be wise for us to put off further conversation on the matter for the present. I shall say no more."

The bishop employed his linen to wipe away a tear. Between sniffles, he declared, "My dear child, I know what you are thinking—that I shall change my mind. But I do not intend to change it. Mr. Aycock states that Ryder has been guilty of crimes against morality, and as bishop, I am obliged to cry out against him. Therefore, even if your mother were to descend from Heaven this moment and instruct me to forgive him, I could not do it." He blew his nose.

"I expect you have forgotten how persuasive Mama was."

His head snapped up and he blanched. "Well, I should not *defy* her, precisely. She was not a woman to be defied, was she? She was always very knowledgeable and performed any task she addressed in the most excellent manner. Naturally, I treasured her advice and counsel and always followed it, without fail."

"Of course, you did. Nobody thinks otherwise. Calm yourself, Papa."

"But now I think on it, I doubt I should have to defy her in this matter, for she never approved of my chaplains' falling in love with you and would certainly not approve of Mr. Starr's doing so. The fellow has no income, no position and no connections, at least none who will recognize him. A most unsuitable match, my dear. No, she would not like it at all. Nor would she insist on my forgiving a gentleman whom I took to my bosom and regarded as a son, while he, in his turn, intended nothing less than to use me for his own nefarious purposes. Forgiveness is all well and good and what we are enjoined to do in the Scriptures, but, she would say, it must not be carried to excess. I am certain she would not wish me to be overzealous in forgiveness."

"Your pride is wounded, Papa. You are angry now. But I have every hope you will recover, for you love him well."

"No! He has gone too far." A succession of sniffles and hiccups escaped him. "The boy has fairly broke my heart, and he will break yours as well, my dear. Mark my words."

Aurora put her arm through her father's to lead him from the room. "Come, I shall have Nussle bring you a cup of chocolate and a helping of ginger cake. You will feel ever so much better."

"Ah, yes," he said as he permitted himself to be coaxed out the door, "that would be most comforting, but I do not intend to change my mind."

"Of course not, Papa. Not tonight, at any rate."

"Not tonight. Not ever."

THE CONSTABLE ESCORTED Mr. Starr to the jailer's lodgings, where Mr. Gunion sat in the single available chair, eating a meal of coarse bread, ham, potato and beer. Chewing rapidly, he set aside his tin plate and welcomed the new occupant of his jail, removing the gargantuan bib he had tied round his neck and apologizing for the indistinctness of his words, as he still had a mouthful of dinner.

The constable introduced his prisoner, charged the jailer to be civil, as Mr. Starr was a gentleman, and took himself off. Forgetting where he had put his bib, Mr. Gunion wiped his mouth on his sleeve, bowed and begged pardon for the condition of the jail. "It is fair dusty, your worship," he acknowledged. "We've had no guests this fortnight, since the last assize, when all the prisoners wuz taken out and hung."

This last word induced Mr. Starr to pause in his inspection of the place and to consider what might lie in store for him.

"If you would be so good as to come this way, your worship, I shall make you what comfort I can."

He led Mr. Starr to a cell at the far end of the room. It was empty, save for a cot with a thread-worn blanket of no discernible colour. Mr. Gunion pulled open the door, which was constructed of heavy wood with a barred window at the top, and gestured politely to his prisoner to enter.

Mr. Starr strolled inside as though he had entered a grand ballroom. He looked about him with curiosity and, searching in his pocket, removed the last coin he had to his name and placed it in Mr. Gunion's hand. He smiled, saying, "I fear I have interrupted your supper."

Awed by this politeness, Mr. Gunion hesitated. Then, apparently on impulse, he drew out a soiled handkerchief from his pocket and employed it to dust the cot. "There, now your worship may sit," he said.

Mr. Starr sat. On three sides of the cell he saw grey walls, roughly plastered over and stained with yellow. The floor was bare and creaky. There was no window, not even a table or a chair. The poverty and bleakness of his surroundings suited him well, he thought.

"Mr. Gunion, you are too kind," he said. "What a pity there is no basin. I should have liked to wash. I have been travelling, you see, and have had no time to make myself presentable."

"Ah, but there is a basin, if I can find where I put it last. That is to say, it is properly a bucket, not a basin. But I shall go and fill it at the pump and ye shall wash to ye'r heart's content." He started to exit the cell when Mr. Starr called him back.

"You have forgotten your handkerchief," he said, handing it to him with eminent politeness.

Mr. Gunion stared. "Ye'r a gentleman to the marrow," he said. "Any other prisoner would have stole the thing." On this, he went out of the cell. Then, pausing abruptly, his hands in his pockets, he said, "Where have I put the blasted thing? It can never be found when it is wanted. Blast. One would think it were a little bit of a thing, for all the days I've mislaid it, but it's a big brute of a thing, it is."

Mr. Starr tore his eyes from a mouse making tracks across his cell. "Have you lost something, Mr. Gunion?"

"The key. I've mislaid the blasted key again."

"May I help you look for it?"

"Ah, that's kind of your worship, but it'll turn up. It always does."

"You lose it frequently, I collect."

"Near every day. It is the most remarkable thing, nary a day goes by that I don't disremember where I've put it." He laughed and shrugged. "A confounded habit for a jail keeper, I vow!"

Mr. Starr could not help smiling. "Well then, I shall wait until you have found it to have my bucket of water."

"Ye'll not wait another minute. I shall go and fill it at the pump just outside, and you will give me your promise not to escape and I shall take your word on it as a gentleman."

"After today, you may be the last man in Sudsbury to believe the word of a gentleman."

"That's as may be, sir, but have I your promise not to try and escape?"

"Mr. Gunion, where on earth would I go?"

"Then you will stay! I thank ye, sir." And off he went on his mission.

Mr. Starr regarded the open door for some time. He had no intention of escaping; he was weary and, besides, had given his word. But he did not like to leave the door open, as though he were inviting anybody and everybody to walk in at will. Not that a fellow in his circumstances was likely to be entertaining a great many visitors. Still, he wished to have privacy; he needed to think.

After pulling the door shut with a clang, he lay back on the cot and watched a mouse disport itself with a crumb before disappearing into the floorboards. Putting his hands behind his head, he inspected the ceiling and cursed himself for a fool. "Ryder, old fellow," he said aloud, "you are a conceited, corkbrained, addlepated nodcock, that's what you are. You will be ousted from the fraternity of rogues, and it is no more than you deserve."

Bitterly, he recollected coming into his chamber and catching sight of Aurora. She had been sitting demurely on his bed, watching him with her large eyes, looking for all the world like the definition of exquisiteness. He had assumed she had come to welcome him, that she had missed him, that she had been unable to wait to receive him properly in the parlour, but had braved scandal and come to his room. When he had gazed into her eyes, he had read love. When she had gaped at the sight of his bare chest, he had read love. When she had permitted him to graze her lips and her neck with his mouth, he had read love. Oxford would have been ashamed of his illiteracy, he told himself: he had misread every syllable.

Lovesickness had blinded him to logic. Thus, he had overlooked the fact that she could have had no notion of the day of his return, let alone the hour. She could not possibly have been there to welcome him.

On the contrary, the opposite had been true. He had taken her by surprise. She had not come to see him, but to spy on him. In point of fact, seeing him was the last thing she had wished. She had read Mr. Aycock's letter and was searching among his things for proof of his perfidy. That was what she had wanted: to pin him to the wall. She cared no more for him than his uncle had done.

The bishop had been in on the scheme, too. Perhaps the coachman had given him early word of his return, so that while the daughter had occupied him with kisses—the thought of which even now impelled him to loosen his collar—the father had caused the constable to be summoned. It had all been neatly done, he granted them that. If he ever got out of the Sudsbury jail, he would never underestimate the formidableness of a pair of innocents.

He was roused from these cheerless thoughts by a clamour at the jail door. It swung open, letting a hint of summer-evening breeze enter through the bars of his cell, and along with it, a roar of voices—ladies' voices.

Rising, he approached the door. Filling the jailer's lodgings was a feminine throng, twenty or thirty strong, and looking none too pleased. At their head stood Mrs. Bludthorn and the other members of the Ladies' Book Society, with one exception—Aurora was not present.

Mrs. Bludthorn looked about, put her linen to her nose as though she smelled a three-day fish, and approached the door. She glared at Mr. Starr. "Is it true, sir," she demanded without preamble, "that you have embezzled two hundred pounds from the diocese?"

Impressed by the degree to which rumour had inflated his crime, he replied, "No, ma'am. I have been accused of misappropriating two pounds sixpence."

Somewhat disappointed by the unheroic proportions of the sum, the lady enquired, "Why did you steal it, sir? Are you so desperate that you could not trust your friends to aid you in your straitened circumstances? Did you think we would turn you away?"

"Madam, I had on my person diocesan funds to pay Mr. Horner for repairs on the church at St. Cuthbert's. I used a portion of the money to purchase gardening implements and seed for Mrs. Horner. I intended to make up the expenditure out of my pocket as soon as I received my first quarter's salary. I informed the bishop of the entire proceeding, and at the time, he did not indicate that he thought I had behaved improperly."

"And why should we believe you, sir?"

"I cannot think of a reason, except that it is the truth."

"Do you have a witness? Mr. Nussle, perhaps?"

Mr. Starr's lips tightened as he thought of Aurora. She might vouch for the truth of what he said, but he would die sooner than put himself at her mercy. He answered simply,

"Mr. Nussle is entirely blameless. He knew nothing of these events."

The Dickery twins now insinuated themselves among the bodies that continued to squeeze into the room to hear the cross-examination. One of them asked breathlessly, "Is it true, Mr. Starr, that you meant to elope with Mrs. Horner to Gretna Green?" Her sister added just as breathlessly, "And is it true you meant to take her children along as well?"

In his time, Mr. Starr had envisioned many an amorous adventure, and he had transformed a goodly number of them into reality, but never had it occurred to him, even in a mere vision, to run off with a harried mother and confine himself in a carriage with her brood all the way to Scotland. Therefore, he was able to reply with perfect truth, smiling only a little, "I ask you, ladies, would Mrs. Horner agree to leave her worthy husband for the likes of me? Would any of you?"

Judging by the expressions they wore, they would have, and so he was required to amend his answer. "That good lady has far too much sense and virtue to abandon her duties, as you all do."

"Your answer, then, is that there was no thought of elopement?"

"Yes."

The baron's widow pushed forward now to ask, "Is it true, Mr. Starr, that you fabricated the tale of your Fontinella?"

He rolled his eyes, wishing devoutly that he had never heard that deuced name. "Yes, it is true," he stated, "and I hope this confession will put an end once and for all to the lady who has haunted me since I first heard her unfortunate appellation."

This answer produced a buzz throughout the room. "In other words," the widow said accusingly, "you were never engaged to her and she is not dead, as you claimed."

"Exactly so."

"Then it is true what they say! Your Fontinella is in truth alive, an actress on the stage at the Haymarket, and you keep her in a well-appointed house in Chelsea, and have bought her an emerald with the money you raised for the Samaritan Hospital!"

Though his position was a desperate one, Mr. Starr was forced to laugh. "Ladies, had I known that being sent to jail afforded so much amusement, I should never have avoided it so assiduously."

Before the women could press him to make a more specific answer, the door pushed open. A path parted through the centre of the crush, in a manner that resembled the parting of the Red Sea. Instead of Moses, however, Nussle came forward, bearing a cloth-covered tray. When he reached the cell, he turned to the crowd to admonish it. "Ladies, I am able to assure you that Mr. Starr will be released as soon as this regrettable misunderstanding is put to rights. Therefore, you may go about your business and let the gentleman have his dinner."

Nobody stirred.

Unwilling to waste any more time reasoning with such a collection of dunces, Nussle turned to his master. "Where is the jailer, sir? I must ask him to open the door."

"Permit me, Nussle. Mr. Gunion has kindly afforded me every opportunity to entertain visitors." So saying, Mr. Starr swung open the door to his cell and invited the butler inside.

Nussle was followed into the cell by as many ladies as would fit.

"Merciful Heaven!" Mrs. Bludthorn exclaimed. "There is not a stick of furniture in here."

"It is awfully drab," pronounced the Dickery twins.

The widow of the baron added, "The place has mice. It is full of droppings."

Immediately, a consultation was held to decide what to do about Mr. Starr's lamentable accommodations at the jail.

Meanwhile, Nussle set the tray down on the cot and encouraged the prisoner to eat. "The young lady had the tray sent over," he said.

"Miss Valentin, you mean?"

"She is in a state of great alarm over your situation."

"No doubt she is. She fears I will either escape or be exonerated."

Nussle pushed out his bottom lip. "You mistake her, sir. Even as we speak, she is endeavouring to persuade the bishop to reconsider the charge."

"I dare say she thinks she has enough evidence against me, without resorting to an unfounded accusation of thievery. She would not like the bishop to be brought up on charges of bearing false witness." He sat on the cot with the tray on his lap and peeked under the cover. In addition to food, the tray contained a book: Aurora's copy of *Persuasion*.

Nussle, who had heard Mr. Starr's words in consternation, shook his head. "I beg pardon for contradicting, sir. I believe I know my place better than to speak when I ought to keep mum. However, I am shocked to discover how abysmally you have misconstrued the young lady's intentions."

"Humble as ever, I see, Nussle. You really must learn not to be so reticent in the expression of an opinion." He inspected the cold beef and jellied sauce.

"You implied, sir, that Miss Valentin meant to harm you. I assure you, nothing could be further from her thoughts."

Gesturing with the drumstick of a roasted fowl, Mr. Starr replied, "I agree with you completely. The young lady never *meant* harm. She did harm out of the best of intentions."

Mr. Nussle was momentarily jostled by the ladies, who were measuring the length and breadth of the cell with an eye to decorating it suitably for habitation by a gentleman. When he had regained his dignity, he said, "I do not understand."

Mr. Starr set aside the tray and rose. In a low voice that emphasized the force of his emotion, he said, "Miss Valentin puts me much in mind of my uncle, Nussle. Like his late lordship, the young lady is possessed of good intentions. The only difficulty is that the intended good produces evil. In the case of my uncle, the evil arose from carelessness and neglect. He meant to do good—he simply did not get round to it. In the case of Miss Valentin, the evil arose from a desire to know the truth, estimable in itself, but devastating to me and my cause."

"What truth?"

"The truth about Ryder Starr. You see, she wrote to Mr. Aycock. From him she learned of our scoundrelly escapades throughout the nation. And she wrote to my cousin as well, prompting him to send for me to announce that I shall never see a groat from my uncle's estate, no matter how many schemes I devise to force him to cough up the blunt, nor how often I remind him of his father's express wishes."

This speech was too much for Nussle. He took a step back. However, he had no place to go, every inch of the cell being occupied by ladies in the throes of wondering how curtains might be mounted to prettify prison bars.

Seeing that he had shocked the butler, Mr. Starr collected himself and endeavoured to appear more sanguine.

"Never mind, old friend. It will all be well. Mr. Gunion can never find the key to this place, and so if it appears they mean to imprison me for any length of time, I shall simply be off. But I take my oath not to leave Sudsbury before paying you a visit and allowing you to scold me one last time, and so you need not be alarmed on my behalf."

Nussle did not return his smile. Tightly, he said, "I shall be alarmed if I choose, sir. Although Fate has allotted me an inferior position in society, I am a free man and believe myself to be in full possession of my faculties. I know when it is fitting to be alarmed and when it is not. If I choose to be alarmed, I shall be alarmed, regardless of what others may command me to do." Here he stood straight and bit his lip.

"Damn!" Mr. Starr murmured. "I wish you would not be so loyal."

"If I choose to be loyal, sir, that is none of your affair, begging your pardon, sir." With the briefest of nods, Nussle turned and pushed his way through the ladies to the door. After some struggle, he contrived to open it and came face to face with Mr. Gunion, who peered inside with curiosity.

"You run a ramshackle jail," the butler informed him with asperity. "You had better see to it at once!"

Mr. Gunion watched him stride elegantly out of the jail, then, shaking his head, made his way into the thickness of ladies, carrying in front of him a sloshing bucket.

Indicating the visitors, Mr. Gunion observed to his prisoner, "I see you are nicely settled, your worship."

Mr. Starr nodded and whispered, "I do hope you will soon find the key, Mr. Gunion. I do not wish to be an unappreciative guest, but I require my privacy, and I had thought that if there was one place where a fellow might shut out the world and its cares, it was jail."

THE FOLLOWING DAY, after another clamorous visit from
the ladies and a stately one from Nussle, Mr. Starr at last
found himself quite alone. Mr. Gunion had had his dinner
sent up from The Three Crowns and was digesting it with a
peaceful nap in his chair. Mr. Starr was thus at liberty to
enjoy his privacy to the utmost. Instead of pleasure, though,
he experienced a hollow sensation that he could not immediately identify. After a time, he wondered if it might be regret or, perhaps, loneliness. Shaking it off, whatever it was,
he opened *Persuasion* at the page he had marked. His eye
fell on a paragraph:

> I can listen no longer in silence. I must speak to you by
> such means as are within my reach. You pierce my soul.
> I am half agony, half hope. Tell me not that I am too
> late, that such precious feelings are gone forever. I of-
> fer myself to you again with a heart even more your
> own than when you almost broke it....

He clapped the book shut, flung it at the wall and con-
signed all female authors to hell. Damn those women! They
could think of nothing better to prattle about than love,
which was, at best, a faradiddle of treacly drivel, and, at
worst, the undoing of a man. He was heartily sick of love.

Hearing someone enter the jail, he came alert.

"May I visit the prisoner?" a voice asked.

"Go right in, miss," Mr. Gunion invited. "The door an't
locked. I still han't found the blasted key."

Before Mr. Starr could prevent it, Aurora entered his cell.

They looked at one another so long that he thought the
metal bars would melt. Then she glanced down and said, "I
am glad you are not treated as a common felon. I hope you
are comfortable." She looked at the elegant writing table
that Mrs. Bludthorn had sent, the chair and its cushion, a

gift from the Dickery twins, the pile of quilts and blankets the widow and her neighbours had brought, and the scattering of pictures of dogs, horses and pastoral scenes that had been affixed to the exposed beams.

"Exceedingly comfortable, thanks to the Ladies' Book Society and their acquaintance." He lounged against a wall, his arms folded, regarding her in the manner he reserved for ladies whom he wished to stare out of countenance.

The device succeeded; Aurora could not meet his gaze. She shifted about uneasily and said, "It appears there is nothing you lack, nothing I may do for you."

"I do not require your charity, if that is what you mean."

"That is not what I mean!" she flared.

He smiled and watched as she strove to recover her equanimity. It pleased him that she could not feign easiness, whereas it was second nature to him.

"I am not here on a mission of charity," she said.

"But of course you are. You find my position pitiable. It quite stirs your compassionate heart, so much so that you have resolved to establish the Samaritan Hospital for Gentleman Rogues and Other Unfortunate Males of Criminal Disposition. Naturally, you wish me to be the first to take advantage of this peerless opportunity to be reformed."

"I do not think you are of a criminal disposition!"

"Then why did you write to Mr. Aycock, pray tell? Why did you write my cousin? Why did you steal into my bedchamber? Was it because you trusted me and believed me to be a gentleman of the most estimable character?"

Blushing ferociously, Aurora said, "We have both been very wrong, to be sure. For my part, I am deeply sorry."

"Why should you be sorry? You were right. You ought to enjoy it!"

Her breath seemed to catch in her throat. He thought at first that the blush of her complexion would resolve itself in tears. Somehow, though, she surprised him, and instead of dissolving, she said with an effort, "We have more important matters at hand."

"What could be more important, Miss Valentin, than deciding which of us is the more gifted beguiler?"

She inhaled. "Your life, Ryder. It is more important to me than anything."

He frowned and turned away, leaning his hand against the wall so that she would be unable to see the emotion on his face.

"Are you aware that you are accused of a capital crime, that because you are supposed to have stolen in excess of twelve pence, you could be sentenced to death by hanging?"

He did not move.

Her voice became more urgent. "Justice Conkle assures me that it is unlikely you will hang. But he thinks you may be transported."

He gave no sign of having heard.

"Ryder, you will perish in exile at Botany Bay!"

Nodding slightly, he said, "You are right. You did not come on a mission of charity. You are here to gloat."

She stamped her foot. "I am here to inform you that I have written to Mr. Benjamin Puissant of London. Although he is not a barrister, he will be able to counsel you."

"Ah, my old friend Mr. Puissant. I wish you had not troubled him."

"I do not intend to see you die on the gallows or be sent away to die of disease and deprivation."

"But surely," he said with an ironic smile, "you wish to see justice prevail."

"A sentence of transportation would not be justice. It would be cruelty. You are innocent, and though you may wish to make yourself out to be a villain, I know better. I know you.''

Wearily, he turned to face her. "It would be best," he said quietly, "if you were to go away."

It was apparent that this remark smarted; she did not trouble to hide it. "Yes, I shall go away," she said.

Never in his life had he been so desolate to hear a female instantly grant his wish. His jaw tightened. In his imagination, he saw himself striding the three paces that separated them, sliding his arms around her, and kissing her. Instead, he contrived to smile. "I quite understand," he said. "The forthcoming legal proceedings promise to offend the sensibilities of a refined young lady such as yourself. Therefore, it is best that you leave Sudsbury until the worst is over."

She shook her head. "I am going to call on your cousin at Broome Court."

His start was so violent that she stepped back. In a flash, he had her by the arm. "I forbid it."

Silently, she looked at him with a depth he could not fathom. However, he could plainly discern a flicker of pain in her expression, and he realized that once again he had hurt her arm. Setting his teeth, he took a breath, then pushed her from him.

"My cousin is dangerous. You must not go near him. Do you understand? There is no telling what he may do."

"He must know that you require his help. At the very least, I may prevail upon him to pay the two pounds six-pence. I should have paid it myself, only my father would not accept it from me. The Ladies' Book Society and others have offered to pay it as well. Indeed, they collected twenty-four pounds to cover the debt, but Justice Conkle will not accept it until he learns more of the case. The charge has been laid before him in form, he says, and he does not like to go to all that trouble for nothing. I expect it is my father's influence, too, that prevents him from accepting the money. But if Lord Matchless will use his influence to your benefit, I believe the sum might be paid."

He strove to keep from touching her, saying coolly, "When I met with him, Frederick was drunk and half out of his mind. He threw me against the wall and would have beaten me senseless if I had not been stronger and quicker. I warn you, Aurora, he will not hesitate to hurt you. Do not think your sex will protect you from attack."

She nodded. "I shall be certain to remember that. I thank you for the warning."

"I do not want you to thank me! I want you to change your mind. This is my affair. Stay out of it."

For a brief time, she considered his words. It had been a first principle with her not to interfere in the affairs of others, especially those she loved. But this was no time for adhering to lofty principles. People's lives were at stake; that is to say, Mr. Starr's life was at stake. She moved to the door. "I shall send Nussle with your supper," she said.

He went to her, and would have taken her arm again, but checked himself. "Swear to me that you do not mean to go to Broome Court."

It seemed she would weep, for she pressed her hand to her mouth. Then, suddenly, she let her hand fall and stood on tiptoe to kiss him on the lips. Before he could collect himself, she was out the door. It clanged shut, followed by the unfamiliar sound of the key turning in the lock. When he went to the bars to look out, Mr. Gunion beamed at him. "The young lady is gone, sir," he announced, "but the key is here. Yes, it has showed herself to me, just as I knew it would. I only hope the next time as it's lost, it won't be when your worship is inside, for then we'll have the devil's own time getting you out again."

THIRTEEN: The Angel of Death

DRESSED IN BONNET and travelling cloak, Aurora opened the door to the bishop's chambers to find her father sitting at his desk with his head in his hands. When he heard her enter, he looked up. His cheeks shone with tears.

"What have I done?" he implored.

She came close and touched a comforting hand to his shoulder. "It will all be well," she said, though her voice did not sound as confident as her words.

"I have wronged the poor boy, Aurora, and it is too late. The harm is already done. How vexed your mother will be with me; I have made a shambles of the business. I would have left everything in her hands, if only I could. I fear it is all up with us now, child."

"Do not despair, Papa," she said gently. "It is very simple. You will pay Ryder his salary—even though it is not yet the end of the quarter—and then you will prevail upon Justice Conkle to accept the payment."

Woefully, he shook his head. "Meanwhile the poor boy wastes away in jail, with the rats and the cold and the damp, and if he does not take a chill and die before we have done, he will be transported or hanged, and it is all my fault."

"No, Papa, it will not come to that. Why, even if it is necessary for him to stand trial, you may testify on his behalf."

The bishop spread his arms helplessly. "I shall do all of it—pay out his quarter's salary, exhort the justice, testify, if it comes to that, but it will be useless, my dear. My changing my mind will not free Ryder from jail, for, you see, Mr. Aycock and his fellows have sent a letter of warning. They mean to arrive at the earliest possible moment to charge him with fraud. If he were not in jail already, thanks to me, he soon would be in any case, and they mean to have his head on a plate. Oh, what are we to do, Aurora?"

She kissed his forehead and said, "You must go to him and tell him you are sorry."

He looked up at her tearfully. "What will that accomplish?"

"It will mean the world to him."

"Will you come with me?"

"I cannot. I have another engagement. But you may take Nussle with you. And the two of you must look after Ryder. Will you promise to look after him, Papa?"

Standing, he said, "My dear, you are trembling. What ails you?"

"You must go to him as soon as possible. You must lose no time in reconciling."

He sighed. "You are right. I cannot put it off. It must be done at once." Gathering up his courage, he made for the door.

As soon as he was gone, Aurora scribbled a note to him on a piece of blank paper. It said that she would return soon, before he was even aware she had gone, and that he was not to fret. To make certain the latter instruction might be more easily carried out, she did not tell him where it was she meant to go.

SINCE AURORA'S DEPARTURE, Mr. Starr had spent his time pacing his cell like a caged tiger, thinking how he might stop her. When he heard the key in the lock and the murmur of voices outside his cell, he stopped, buoyed by the hope that she had changed her mind and had returned to tell him so. But, in an instant, the bishop stood before him, and, looming tall behind him, was Nussle. The two of them appeared as sombre as a tomb.

Mr. Starr's agitation rose in proportion to his disappointment. He recovered himself quickly, however, thinking that next to Aurora's own large brown and trusting eyes, there were no two sights he would rather see, for they could assist him. "I am glad you have come," he said. "We must find a way to stop her."

"I have come to ask your forgiveness, my boy," said the old man with dignity.

Rapt in his thoughts, Mr. Starr resumed pacing. "You must go and talk to her at once. I doubt she will pay you any heed at first, for she is deucedly determined, but she must be brought to listen. She must!"

"Perhaps you did not hear me, dear boy. I have come to beg pardon. I was wrong, very wrong."

"Even if she has already set out, she might easily be overtaken by a man on horseback. It is not too late. It cannot be too late."

"I can see you do not wish to speak to me. You are angry, and I have no right to expect otherwise. But I shall do what I may to make it up to you, Ryder."

The poor bishop might as well have spoken to the walls so lately ornamented by the Ladies' Book Society, for Mr. Starr was entirely engrossed in thoughts of Aurora. "The best way is to find a horseman," he mused. "A man on horseback is sure to overtake her if we do not waste another moment. Unfortunately, Nussle cannot abide an animal, and you, Bishop, must travel by carriage. Somehow, we must find a horseman."

Thunderously, Nussle cleared his throat. "Master Ryder, mind your manners, if you please. The bishop is addressing you."

Mr. Starr stopped pacing. It occurred to him that Nussle was right—the bishop was talking to him. He had not heard a word. "Good day to you, Bishop," he said.

Tears prevented the old man from repeating his plea. Instead, he approached Mr. Starr and clasped him in his arms. The bishop was only a little more than half the younger man's size, and his chubby arms scarcely reached round him, but the gesture was enough to pierce Mr. Starr's composure. All his emotion, which had previously been caught up in preoccupation with Aurora's safety, now flooded over him. He became aware of a hollowness in his chest, as though he had been starved for weeks. After keeping himself stiff for a time, he moved an awkward hand to pat the bishop's back, while, over the man's shoulder, he regarded Nussle with an expression of wonder.

Discreetly, Nussle inspected a faded portrait of a hound.

When the bishop stepped back and wiped away a tear, Mr. Starr found himself shaken. The old man persisted in reminding him of his uncle, and it was the most confounded nuisance, for he had no time for nostalgia. He must find a way to stop Aurora.

"Will you forgive me, my boy?"

"Certainly, if you will forgive me."

This complaisance was received with a beaming smile. "Then we shall forgive each other! Oh, how very relieved I am. And now, if Mrs. Valentin will forgive us both, we shall all live happily ever after." He wiped his eyes.

"We do not quite have a happy ending yet, I fear. We must first prevent your daughter from getting herself in the devil of a pickle."

The bishop blinked.

Nussle frowned.

Mr. Starr explained. "She intends to visit Broome Court. She has some ridiculous notion that she can persuade my cousin to intercede with the law on my behalf. Not only is she gone on a fool's errand, but she is putting herself in the gravest jeopardy. There is no telling what harm my cousin Matchless may do."

"He would not hurt her!" the bishop cried.

Nussle wagged his head. "Ah, Bishop, far be it from me to utter a word to the detriment of my betters," he lamented, "but Lord Matchless has had a vile temper ever since he was a lad. He was wont to throw kittens in the pond and tear the heads off grasshoppers whenever he was displeased. The only time he laughed was when one of the servants was scolded."

"Oh, dear," the bishop said. "And Aurora's gone to pay him a call. I do wish she had not."

"I mean to stop her," Mr. Starr said.

Nussle gazed around the cell. "I do not see how, unless Mr. Gunion can contrive to misplace the key again, and very soon."

With a smile, Mr. Starr remarked, "It occurs to me that, with the bishop's assistance, such a loss might easily occur."

"I have not the least idea what it is you wish me to do," said the bishop, "but I am ready to do it at a moment's notice and will not falter! We must save Aurora at all costs."

"I should not hesitate to put your stalwart resolution to the test, Bishop, but for one difficulty. You see, we cannot place Mr. Gunion in the position of having allowed his prisoner to escape. If it does not make him appear negligent in the extreme, it will bring him an accusation of bribe-sucking. Either way, he would be dismissed at once. No, we must devise a scheme that will place all the blame for the escape at my door.''

Nussle objected, ''But Master Ryder, if you are blamed, you might end by being hanged.''

Mr. Starr smiled wryly. ''I am already charged with a hanging offence, Nussle. If the law must have its full complement of vengeance, it is welcome to hang me twice.''

As THE BELL-PULL at Broome Court did not raise an answer, and as the knocker had come loose from its moorings, Aurora was obliged to have the coachman pound on the door. It opened to reveal a worn and weary Mrs. Verbost who wiped her hands on her pinafore and complained, ''I am now to do the office of footman, I suppose! The servants have all been turned off, and I am virtually alone, and if 'twere not that I remembered the old Lord Matchless that was, I should run off myself in the blinking of an eye!''

Having listened politely to this effusion, Aurora said, ''Will you kindly tell his lordship that Miss Aurora Valentin has come to call.''

Mrs. Verbost pursed her lips and regarded her as though she were a fanciful child. ''His lordship does not receive visitors,'' she said. ''And this is no place for a proper young lady such as yourself. You must climb into your fine carriage and go back where you came from, and if I had a particle of sense, I should do the same.''

''Thank you,'' Aurora said. ''You are very kind, but I shall not go away until I have seen Lord Matchless.''

The housekeeper would have argued further, but there was a firmness in Aurora's expression that persuaded her otherwise. She stared at the young woman in uncertainty.

''I come on Mr. Starr's behalf,'' she said.

"Master Ryder?" Anxious curiosity replaced Mrs. Verbost's disapproving air. "Come inside, then."

In the hall, Aurora was obliged to step round a number of tiles that had come loose from the floor and had not been replaced. She declined to remove her cloak and bonnet and said simply to the housekeeper, "Mr. Starr is in jail, and I must enlist his cousin's aid in freeing him."

Mrs. Verbost gasped. "Jail! Oh, the poor lad. But it is no use your coming here, miss. That one will never lift a finger to help a soul, and certainly not Master Ryder. He's hated the sweet boy since he first showed his face in this ill-fated house."

Aurora had resolved to permit nothing to deter her. Accordingly, she said, "I believe this is a predicament that goes beyond like and dislike. His lordship will not wish a near blood relation to be brought before the bench. He will not wish to see the name of Matchless tarnished. Nor will he wish to place himself in the despicable light of one who refuses to take action for the sake of his family."

Mrs. Verbost sighed. "It appears logical enough, miss, but his lordship is not in a way to like logic."

"Will you allow me to speak to him?"

"I do not know as I ought."

"Please."

"He is not to be trusted, miss. Did Master Ryder not warn you?"

"Yes, he warned me, but I must make the attempt. You see, I love your Master Ryder and must do what I may for him."

The housekeeper flushed with pleasure. "In that case, I shall show you the way."

"Thank you." They started along the shabby hall.

"Do not thank me, miss," said the housekeeper, "for I shan't permit you to go inside alone. I shall send for some gentlemen of the town, and they will protect you. You ought not to have come unprotected, you know. If you like, I shall fetch one of the old lord's pistols."

"Thank you but that is unnecessary. It is better that I come unprotected. Lord Matchless is less likely to believe himself threatened, and therefore less likely to do me an injury, if I am clearly without weapon or guard."

Mrs. Verbost stopped before the door to the library. Putting her ear to the door, she listened. "I hear nothing," she whispered.

"I shall go inside."

"Will you not reconsider?"

By way of answer, Aurora turned the handle and pushed the door open. She glanced briefly at the housekeeper, then turned to face the dim room. The sudden closing of the door behind her made her swallow hard.

Aurora was wholly unprepared for what she saw: a raven-haired gentleman who might have perfectly resembled Ryder Starr if he had not looked so haggard and wild, sitting on the carpet, surrounded by books. They lay everywhere, covering the tables, chairs, rugs, and corners. Most of them were either open, torn, or both. The shelves stood half-empty.

An enormous lexicon rested in his lordship's lap. Painstakingly, he turned over the pages one by one. Because he took no notice of her entrance, Aurora drew near and cleared her throat. Still he demonstrated no consciousness of her presence, and so she knelt by his side.

"You are reading, sir?"

"I am looking," he said, without removing his eyes from the leaves of the book.

"Perhaps I may be of help." She seized a weighty tome and began leafing through it. "May I ask what it is we are looking for?"

"You will know when you see it."

"It is a certain piece of information, I collect."

"Yes. It is here. I know it is here somewhere, for I put it here with my own hands."

"Would it disturb our search, do you think, if I told you why I have come?"

"Do as you like. It is a matter of indifference to me."

For a time, they turned pages in silence. Then, when she had summoned her courage, Aurora said, "You must wish to know who I am."

For the first time, he looked at her. His eyes, like Mr. Starr's, were black. But instead of glowing with a teasing light, they were lifeless. "I know who you are," he said.

Aurora sat back. "You know me?"

"Of course. You are the Angel of Death."

He spoke in a child's voice, and Aurora could not help but pity him. His condition was so appalling that she felt even Ryder would have pitied him. The man's hair was a mass of tangles, as though he had not put a comb to it in months. Unwashed, unkempt, he smelled of drink and sickness.

Setting aside the book, Aurora put her hand on his arm. "May I entreat you, my lord, to eat something? There is a tray just over there. Perhaps you will allow me to assist you."

"I am not hungry."

"You are weak. It appears to me that some nourishment would revive you."

"I do not wish to be revived."

"If you ate a few morsels, your search would be more successful. You would return to it refreshed."

This argument appeared to sway him. He allowed her to help him to a chair. After she had lowered him into it, she fetched the tray. Inspecting its contents, she found that the fruit and bread and butter were reasonably fresh. Because the table was piled with books, she set the tray on his knees. After she had sliced a morsel of bread, she knelt and endeavoured to tempt him to eat.

"I should prefer not to go with you at this time," he said to her in a weary voice. "I should like to find what I have been looking for, and then you may take me."

She induced him to taste a bit of bread. "I am not an angel, my lord, and I have not come to take you. I am Aurora Valentin, who wrote to you not long ago, and I am here on behalf of your cousin, Mr. Starr."

He grew rigid. "I cannot escape the fellow. Even Death will not grant me relief from him."

"Your assistance is needed, and there is not a moment to lose. He has been imprisoned. If you will exert your influence, you may prevent the rankest injustice, and you will save the name of Matchless from untold damage."

"Get away."

So low was his tone that she did not catch his words. "I beg your pardon?" she said.

"Get away!" he shrieked, forcing her, in her surprise, to fall back. His eyes shone like an inky whirlpool, and though Aurora knew his state of health and mind had rendered him perilously unpredictable and though she was frightened, she was not about to be frightened off. Slowly, she rose. With difficulty, she found a little space to stand amidst the stacks of books. Taking a deep breath, she stated, "I have come to obtain your assistance. I shall not go away until I have succeeded."

"Damn you!" The cry echoed in the half-empty shelves and lingered just below the arched ceiling. "Damn him!" In his frenzy, he threw the tray from his lap, and, reaching down, lifted a handful of books. "Go away." He spoke with menace, then hurled a book at her head. Despite his weak condition, it was well aimed. More books came at her, so that she was forced to put up her hands to shield her face. She cried out in protest as one of the volumes grazed her bonnet and another hit her leg. Backing away, she tripped on an array of books and nearly fell. A book hit her in the chest, and she heard her attacker laughing.

No wonder Ryder had demanded that she stay away from Broome Court, she thought. How wilful she had been to ignore his warning. How perverse of her to have chosen such a moment to interfere in the concerns of another!

But there was no time to consider the valuable lessons one might learn from being proved royally wrong. Books were flying at her now, and she was scarcely able to dodge them. She did not dare turn her head to calculate the distance to the door or the desk. All she could do was evade the missiles that, judging by his lordship's oaths, were intended to kill her.

Then they stopped. Lord Matchless cried in an agony of joy, "There it is!" His arms reaching towards her, he attempted to rise from his chair but could not. With a groan, he slumped back.

Before her was a piece of paper. It had evidently come loose from one of the books he had thrown and now drifted like a feather toward the floor. Aurora seized it. A brief glance at its title told her that it was a codicil to a will and that it had been written by the father of the present Lord Matchless.

"Give it to me," he said. There was unexpected strength in his tone.

Her thoughts leapt to the housekeeper, who she devoutly hoped had gone after some gentlemen of the town as she had said she would, and that they would appear on the spot to rescue her, for she had no intention of giving up the paper. It was too important to Ryder for her to let it go.

"Bring it here."

She moved forward a step. Inhaling, she took the risk of saying, "Tell me why you have not destroyed it."

Gripping the arms of the chair, he said, "My father gave it to me with instructions to put it into the lawyer's hands at the earliest opportunity. I meant to carry out his wish when he died, but the time never seemed quite right, and so I secreted the thing in a book. As time went on, it seemed impossible to confess that I had kept it, for then I should have been accused of stealing, or worse. But I began to see the paper in my dreams. Its existence preyed on me and would not let me sleep or eat. At last, I determined to deliver it to the lawyer without delay. However, one of the housemaids had disarranged the books during her dusting. Unable to read, she had not set the titles in proper order. Of course, I dismissed the girl at once. Indeed, I dismissed all the servants. But it was too late. I was faced with the necessity of looking through every book in my father's library, and I was too weary and ill for such a task. My cousin did not deserve to inherit anything, and so I was not obligated to find the thing, but I knew that if I did not, I should not know a moment's peace. After a time, even drink brought no solace." He stared at a point in space as though he hoped to read there the explanation for his being so cruelly thwarted.

Aurora listened for the sound of voices outside the library, but heard nothing. She could not remember her conversation with the housekeeper in detail, but she had a vague memory of having asked the woman not to bother to summon the gentlemen of the town. She prayed that Mrs. Verbost had not paid her any mind.

"I will have the paper," his lordship commanded. He twitched; his body would not be still.

It seemed to Aurora that though he was weak, he might yet be furious enough to summon the strength to take it from her. In the process, he would surely rip it to pieces; he might rip *her* to pieces as well. She felt her forehead throb. The quiet in the room made it seem as if nobody would hear her if she screamed. A cunning voice told her to step closer to the man, to pretend that she meant to give him what he wished, but instead, she folded the paper and tucked it in her sleeve.

His face went dark. Putting up a bony finger, he leaned forward, preparing to speak.

Aurora waited for his words. When they did not come, she feared that he meant to attack her physically. He would come at her with his foul breath and his vicious curses. He would suffocate her, his hands squeezing her throat. Breathing hard, she waited. He did not move.

Surprised, she approached him. Although he still seemed about to lurch at her, his strange expression made her more curious than afraid. She drew so near that she might have touched him, but was prevented from doing so by his falling over onto the floor.

In a flash, she was beside him, feeling his wrist for a sign of life. Fear grew in her as the certainty dawned that he was dead. She put her ear to his chest, then sat straight. "No!" she cried, unwilling to permit him to be dead. "You must live! You must help Ryder. What is to become of him if you die?"

From outside the door, she heard her name being called. Then, before she could quite turn round, Ryder was kneeling next to her. He took her hands, chafed them, then held her face. "Are you all right?"

"Lord Matchless is dead," she told him.

He regarded his cousin. "I shall fetch the surgeon." He disappeared so swiftly that Aurora began to doubt he had been there at all. In another moment, he returned with a gentleman—indeed, with a company of gentlemen.

"The doctor has come," Ryder said to her softly.

"Aye," declared Mrs. Verbost, "and the mayor, the law-yer, the baker, the greengrocer and the haberdasher. I've brought them all."

"Come," Ryder said, drawing Aurora to her feet and slipping a supporting arm around her so that she might stand as far from his lordship as possible.

"H'm," Mrs. Verbost said, looking down at the figure of her former master, "I see I ought to have brought the par-son as well."

From her vantage point by the door, Aurora saw the sur-geon examine the fallen man. He looked up at the house-keeper and shook his head gloomily. "I cautioned him, you know. I said that if he continued on his present course, he would drink himself into an early grave, for his heart was weak and his health was failing. And now he has proved me right."

"I, for one, am not surprised," Mrs. Verbost declared. "I prepared him my finest dishes, but he never et a bite."

Aurora looked at Ryder. After pressing her hand heart-eningly, he moved to where his cousin lay and looked down. Though there had been no love lost between the two men, he was obviously pained.

Closing her eyes, Aurora told herself, *I ought never to have interfered.*

How had Ryder come there? she wondered. How had he escaped? Had he escaped for her sake? What would hap-pen to him if he were caught?

She was prevented from asking any of these questions by a shout outside the door and then a crashing noise.

Mr. Gunion burst into the library and stumbled over a mound of books, falling flat at Mr. Starr's feet. Jumping up, he seized the gentleman's arm, shouting at the top of his lungs, "Aha! I have discovered you, you villain! Escape my jail, will you? I shall cart you back to Sudsbury and then you will see what it means to evade the clutches of the law!''

Smiling, Mr. Starr said, ''Mr. Gunion. Why, what a charming surprise to see you here.''

The jailer whispered, ''Did I get it right?''

''Yes, you spoke your lines to perfection, but my cousin is dead and we have no time to act out our little play just now.''

Seeing that most of the inhabitants of the room were gathered round a corpse, Mr. Gunion said, ''It warn't you who did his business for him, I hope. Y'er in trouble aplenty as it stands.''

''Rest easy, Mr. Gunion. This is one offence I am not guilty of.''

''Well,'' said Mrs. Verbost, with practical wisdom, ''I suppose we may as well bury him.''

While the others nodded piously, Mr. Starr glanced round to see how Aurora did. He noted that she leaned back against the wall, her eyes closed. Her complexion was pale, and she scarcely seemed to have noticed Mr. Gunion's unconventional entrance. Witnessing the death of Lord Matchless had obviously shocked her. She would require some time to recover. But she was not hurt. That was the important thing. Unfortunately, he was obliged to return to the jail and was not at liberty to see to her welfare. Collecting himself, he said, ''Mrs. Verbost, will you be so kind as to take Miss Valentin away?''

''I shall make her a pot of tea,'' said the housekeeper. ''After her ordeal, she might do well with a spot of brandy in it.''

He watched them go. Aurora did not look back as she was taken from the library.

Subdued, Mr. Starr turned to Mr. Gunion, saying, "I suppose you may as well escort me back to my cell now. I have accomplished what I came here to do."

"By your leave," said a gentleman, stepping forward. "I do not think it prudent for you to return to jail just now, sir."

Mr. Starr looked the man up and down. "Are we acquainted?" he enquired.

"I am Fletcher Montmercy, Esquire. Allow me to present you with my card."

Taking it and reading, Mr. Starr said, "You are an attorney, I see. Well, if you wish to represent me at my trial, you are welcome to give it a go, but I must warn you, my friend, there exists not a farthing with which to pay you, not a feather to fly with."

Mr. Montmercy chuckled. "You are droll, sir. I do not mean to push myself forward and offer my services as barrister. Oh, no. Quite the contrary. I merely wish to state that you may be in line to succeed your cousin as the Earl of Matchless, and the matter ought to be investigated."

Mr. Starr dragged his hand through his hair. "The new Earl of Matchless!"

"It is quite possible. I am not unfamiliar with your family's situation. You see, I am the successor to Mr. Nitt, your family's late lawyer," Mr. Montmercy explained. "I assisted Mr. Nitt in drawing up your uncle's will."

"I have already heard my uncle's will. As you were concerned in its devising, you will recall that I am not mentioned."

"Yes, but there is no disputing one salient fact, to wit, that you may be the heir to the Matchless monies, estate and lands. And even if you are not the new earl, as a near relation to the deceased and the only relation present, you have certain obligations to tend to immediately, such as the burial of your cousin.''

"But he cannot stay. He is to be hanged!" Mr. Gunion put in.

Mr. Montmercy regarded the jailer as though he were a flea. "It will simply have to wait," he said.

The room buzzed with the news. The sudden demise of the young lord who had been regarded with the liveliest hatred by one and all had caused them to forget momentarily that Mr. Starr might be the successor to the title.

While the others pulled their chins and frowned at him, Mr. Starr laughed at this sudden turn in his fortunes. "Well," he said to them, "my old friend Nussle will be happy to know that I may have come into my inheritance at last. With any luck, I shall not be too dead to enjoy it."

FOURTEEN: Mr. Starr Comes to Judgement

WHEN SHE HAD TAKEN a little tea and sat quietly for some minutes by a fire in the kitchen, Aurora enquired about Mr. Starr. "Is he well?" she asked Mrs. Verbost, who had been running between the library and the kitchen for the past hour.

"As well, I suppose, as any young gentleman can be who must face the gallows or transportation or worse."

"Oh," said Aurora, heartsick that she had come all the way to Worcestershire to save him from that fate and had not only failed to accomplish her purpose but had presided over the death of the only person who could. Regret oppressed her so heavily that she did not know how she would face Ryder again.

But face him she must. The paper in her sleeve must be given to him. Whatever followed next was out of her hands. She was done interfering.

"Is he in the library now?" she asked. "I must speak with him at once."

"Gracious, no, he is long gone from this house, miss. As soon as he gave instructions for the funeral, he was obliged to return to the jail."

Standing like a shot, Aurora said, "But he cannot be gone. I have important news."

"Yes, a pity it surely is that he's gone, seeing as he may be the new lord, and Broome Court is all to pieces and in need of him. What good does he do a body in jail, I should like to know. If the law had any sense, it would let a man speak to the tenants before he was carted off to the hangman's noose."

Only one part of this speech penetrated Aurora's anxiety. "He may be Lord Matchless?"

"Yes, though much good it does him, or any of us."

Hastily, Aurora wrapped herself in her cloak and took her leave. Within minutes, she was installed in her father's carriage and on her way back to Sudsbury as fast as the chestnuts could gallop over the moonlit highway. She must lose no time in speaking with Ryder and preventing the injustice that threatened to take him from her.

In the morning, she sought out her father in the breakfast parlour. He dropped his spoon when he saw her, and it clattered on the plate.

"Thank heaven you are come back. You are unhurt, my dear?"

"Yes, Papa, only I have not succeeded in helping Ryder. Indeed, I have made everything worse."

"You meant well, to be sure."

She stood by the sideboard and gazed tearfully at the delectables it contained. "I do not know what to do for him. I did not even have a moment to see him before he was taken away again."

"We shall go to the jail at once," said her father soothingly. "I shall not even finish this excellent kidney in sauce Nussle prepared for me with his own hands. Ryder is more important than any kidney, after all."

And off they went to the jail, but were unable to obtain any satisfaction, for the prisoner was no longer in residence there. According to Mr. Gunion's report, Mr. Conkle, the Justice of the Peace, would not permit a potential Earl of Matchless to languish in a common jail as though he were

an ordinary criminal. What if Mr. Starr should be declared
the heir? he had argued. He would certainly not look very
kindly upon those who had wronged him, would he? Besides, the justice, who lived quite alone, enjoyed good
companionship over a roasted joint and a bottle and had
found over the years that prisoners in his jail often made
most appreciative guests. Mr. Conkle had caused the prisoner to be brought to his house for dinner. Discovering him
to be a gentleman of education and intelligence, one who,
furthermore, had no objection to playing cards until dawn
every night, he had had Mr. Starr installed in his house. He
had further ordered that no members of the Ladies' Book
Society—indeed, no ladies of any kind, and no person or
persons concerned in the case—be permitted to visit the
prisoner.

The bishop returned to the palace in utter dejection; Aurora was more agitated than ever. How was she to get the
codicil into Ryder's hands? It was imperative that he read it.

No word came of his situation until Nussle, who had
called belowstairs at the justice's house, reported that he did
very well, that the cook and housemaids giggled like fools
over him and were most attentive to his comfort, and that
he entertained himself with whist and with finishing the
novel *Persuasion*. Unfortunately, the justice would not permit his prisoner to receive letters or communications of any
kind before the trial, which, rumour had it, had been set for
a week hence. Forbidden to write or see Ryder, Aurora had
no choice but to wait for the trial.

THE BAILIFF CALLED at the justice's house to escort Mr.
Starr to the Town Hall. To Ryder's amusement, it devel-
oped that his trial was not to be held in the court, but rather
in the vestibule just outside. He was led to a chair that stood
apart from all the others, resembling a makeshift prison-

er's box. Seating himself comfortably, he prepared to be vastly entertained, for the hall swarmed with curiosity-seekers, most of them female, and with his old adversaries from Nardingham and the other towns he had been bribed to leave. The bishop waved to him from the centre of a collection of benches that served as a gallery. On the bishop's left sat Nussle, who ignored the bustle surrounding him and stared ahead with haughty disdain. Aurora sat on her father's right. Her solemn face was unbearably lovely.

"This is not a trial," Justice Conkle explained to the noisy gathering. "It is merely a convocation. I have called it to address the many charges concerning Mr. Starr, so that we may assess whether a trial is in fact warranted. If it is, we may convene at the next assize, and the jury will declare his guilt or innocence. If, in the meanwhile, he should be found to be the Earl of Matchless, he will be tried by his peers and none of us shall need to inconvenience the gentleman further. Heaven knows he has been put to enough trouble already." So saying, he adjusted his wig and sat down behind a large table. Slapping down his fist, he said, "Bailiff, you may declare this convocation in session."

The bailiff obliged, and everybody sat expectantly.

Ryder found himself watching Aurora and caught her once or twice watching him. On the second glance, she essayed a slight smile, which he did not return. Long since, he had forgiven her for being the means of his going to jail, but he could not forgive her for putting her own life in jeopardy. He had known the most acute agony thinking she was in danger. It was one thing for her to dance in a meadow with a schemer or permit a rogue to kiss her in his bedchamber. It was quite another thing for her to visit Frederick Matchless in his library!

His angry expression must have dismayed her, for she looked down at her hands and did not look up again.

Mr. Aycock stood and announced, "Justice, I am, um, come before you today to represent the, um, gentlemen of Nardingham, who have been defrauded by the defendant out of seventy- um, five pounds."

"Don't forget the women," Farmer Guggins reminded him.

"And in addition to said, um, sum," Mr. Aycock continued, "there is the matter of seventeen pounds, which he fleeced the ladies of in the name of a charity—the Samaritan, um, Hospital, which, for all I know, he invented out of the, um, air."

At this accusation, a rotund, balding gentleman rose and declared in a booming voice, "Sir, the Samaritan Hospital is not a fiction but a true and noble institution. Mr. Aycock may go and see it for himself, as it stands here in Sudsbury, and if he does not believe the proof of his own eyes, then he ought not to have the face to call himself a lawyer."

"Who the devil are you?" demanded the justice.

"I am Benjamin Puissant, Esquire, of London, at your service. I am here to confirm that the sum of seventeen pounds was received by the hospital in good form, sent without signature but accompanied by an insignia, a five-pointed star, which I have since learned from witnesses, namely Miss Aurora Valentin and Mr. John Nussle, is the insignia belonging to a gentleman known by the appellation Ryder Starr."

"You are a lawyer?"

"I am so fortunate, yes."

"And you, Aycock, you call yourself a lawyer, too?"

"Um, yes."

"And these gentlemen here, who have come from Up-chalk and other obscure villages, they are lawyers, too?"

"Um, a great many of them are."

Justice Conkle pulled himself to his feet and leaned menacingly over the table. "Out! I will have no lawyers here."

Mr. Puissant stepped back. "I must protest, Justice. How can you hope to have a trial without lawyers?"

"This is not a trial! It is a convocation! And I am not obliged to have any damned lawyers here if I don't wish to! Out!"

Hesitantly, Mr. Aycock said, "Mr. Guggins is a, um, farmer. May he be permitted to, um, stay?"

A stranger jumped up to say, "I am a chandler. Might I be permitted to stay? I paid six shillings to get Mr. Starr out of Clodham."

A chorus of like requests followed from men of every profession and degree, who wished to declare that they were not lawyers and thus entitled to remain in the hall. The cacophony rose to a crescendo, sending Justice Conkle into a fit of red-faced wrath.

"Sit down, all of you," he thundered, "and stop this jingle-brained clatter. I will have order in this court, or rather, this convocation! If you are not as mute as fish this instant, you shall all find yourselves in jail, the whole damned lot of you."

Nobody sat and nobody stopped bellowing, largely because nobody heard a syllable over the din.

Then Mr. Starr stood and cleared his throat. The ladies were first to note that he was on the point of speaking, and so they elbowed and shushed their neighbours.

Bowing elegantly to Mr. Aycock and the others, who had now grown still, he said with a smile, "Gentlemen, what a pleasure to see you all again. How very kind of you to come all the way from Nardingham, Clodham, Littledell and Upchalk merely to attend my trial—that is to say, my convocation. It warms my heart to know you have not forgotten me."

"As like forget a swindler as my own name," muttered Farmer Guggins.

Inclining his head amiably to the farmer, Mr. Starr continued, "I cannot begin to say how much your generous loan of funds has assisted me in my many ordeals since leaving your midst. I am, I hope, not ungrateful, and as Mr. Montmercy has informed me that I may be the heir to a considerable fortune, and may become as scandalously rich as I was formerly scandalously poor, I should like to say that if it does fall out that I am the Earl of Matchless, I shall, as soon as I am able, repay your many kindnesses to me, in full, and with interest."

Mr. Aycock and his fellows regarded Mr. Starr sceptically.

"Who the deuce is this Montmercy fellow?" the justice snapped. "Another lawyer? I vow we have five lawyers for every law!"

Mr. Starr, who had spent upwards of a week with the justice and knew his irascible disposition, continued blithely, "Mr. Montmercy is the gentleman who will convene with Mr. Aycock and the others at the public house, the better to assess the sums owing and to invite them to drink a pot of ale as my guests."

A murmur of approval ran through the gallery. Mr. Starr was pronounced a noble gentleman. If he was not the new earl, surely he ought to be.

Glancing at Aurora, Ryder saw that she remained serious. Everything he had ever taught her about merriment appeared to have been obliterated.

"Quiet!" Justice Conkle commanded. "Now, those of you who wish to have your money and your pint, get out. The rest of you, not a peep."

"Wait!" cried Farmer Guggins, as his comrades rose to follow Mr. Montmercy to the tavern. "What is it we are rushing to do? Shall we content ourselves with promises in lieu of money that justly belongs to us? The rest of you may be foolish enough to hazard the fellow's inheriting a title, but I for one have heard enough of his glib tongue. I will have what is owing to me *now*—and nothing less!"

The other gentlemen, roused by this logic, glared at Mr. Starr, who surmised that his future prospects of good fortune were no more likely than his charm to persuade the buzzards to fly off.

Justice Conkle scratched under his wig, saying, "Your accusers appear to be willing to abandon the case against you, Mr. Starr, but only if they get their blunt in hand."

Affably, Mr. Starr said, "They are all men of honour, Justice, and if they say they wish to have their blunt in hand, then I have no doubt they mean it, and if anybody should accuse any one of them of concealing his true desires, I should be the first to rise to my feet to declare that these are gentlemen who never say what they do not mean, but only what they *do* mean. Unfortunately, I haven't a sou. Prospects, and not greatly rosy ones, are all I possess at the moment." He smiled at his adversaries, waiting to see whether the possibility of regaining their money was sweeter to them than revenge. If the look on their faces was any indication, they vastly preferred the latter.

Aurora rose then, to his surprise and that of everybody else, and said in her musical voice, "May I have a word with you, Justice Conkle?"

The justice, who liked a pretty face almost as much as he liked a hand of cards sprinkled liberally with aces, beckoned to her. "Of course, Miss Valentin," he said silkily. Then, gesturing at the spectators, he snapped, "The rest of you may do as you like."

Apparently what the rest of the onlookers liked was to strain to hear the whisperings at the justice's table.

"Perhaps this will assist Mr. Starr in guaranteeing any payment of funds," she said, pulling Lord Matchless's codicil from her sleeve and, handing it over.

After squinting at its contents, the justice asked, "How did you come by this?"

Clearing her throat, she said, "I called upon the late Lord Matchless at Broome Court, and, quite by accident, it fell into my hands."

The justice announced to one and all, "It appears that regardless of whether Mr. Starr is or is not the Earl of Matchless, he is indeed the heir to a fortune."

Stunned, Mr. Starr stood up. "I must see that paper, Justice."

"All in good time, Mr. Starr. All in good time."

Ryder sat, scarcely able to contain himself. Though he could not see the paper, he sensed its critical nature.

"I have here what purports to be a codicil to Lord Matchless's will, in which Mr. Starr is left the sum of forty thousand pounds."

The announcement of the sum was greeted by a gasp of pleasure. Too often, the onlookers agreed, it was the folks one loathed who came into money. That was not the case here. Mr. Starr's good fortune was welcomed by one and all.

Mr. Starr himself did not utter a sound. Without seeing it for himself, he could not believe that the codicil actually existed, or that Aurora had produced it out of her black bombazine sleeve.

Mr. Aycock frowned. "Why has this, um, codicil only come to light, um, now?"

The justice wrinkled his forehead as he considered this question.

Nussle rose. "I believe I know my place better than to interfere in a proceeding of such a solemn nature as this, but may I be permitted to speak, Justice?"

"Yes, but do not go on about it so. Be brief, man."

"Briefly then, Mr. Starr's cousin, Lord Matchless lately deceased, purloined the codicil." He sat down with a definitive thud.

"How do we, um, know Mr. Nussle is telling the, um, truth?"

"I can corroborate his statement," Aurora said. "Lord Matchless confessed to me that he had withheld the paper, despite his father's request that it be delivered to the lawyer."

"Is the codicil, um, witnessed in proper form?"

"Aye, it looks to be," said the justice.

"Then why have the, um, witnesses not stepped forward to report the existence of a, um, codicil?"

The justice rubbed his chin. "I expect that if Lord Matchless was capable of purloining a codicil, he would not stop at bribing witnesses to keep mum."

A murmur of excitement issued from the crowd. Thievery, bribery—it was quite delicious.

Mr. Montmercy stepped forward then. "May I see the codicil?" he asked.

"Who the devil are you?"

"I am successor to the attorney who drew up Lord Matchless's will. I can verify his lordship's signature, and perhaps those of the witnesses as well."

"Heaven bless us, another lawyer." Wearily, the justice passed him the paper.

While Mr. Montmercy perused it, Ryder sought Aurora's eyes. How the devil had she come by the codicil, he wished to know. What had she suffered at the hands of his cousin to get it? Why would she not look at him? More than anything, more than the money or his uncle's fond words, he wished to see her eyes raised to his.

"These witnesses are dead," Mr. Montmercy declared. "They were taken by the same fever that carried off Lord Matchless. If I recollect, they died within a month of the date upon this document."

"That explains their not stepping forward," said Justice Conkle. "Not even you, Aycock, can fault a dead man for keeping mum."

Mr. Montmercy added, "As the signature greatly resembles that which I have seen on his lordship's will, I have no doubt this will be proved to be a true codicil. Mr. Starr will most certainly be entitled to the aforementioned forty thousand pounds."

As the lawyer from Nardingham had no further arguments to proffer, he shrugged at his fellow creditors.

"What do you think of Mr. Starr's prospects now?" Justice Conkle enquired waspishly.

"They appear to have, um, improved."

"Mr. Aycock," said the justice, "it seems to me that a promise of repayment is better than nothing and not to be sneezed at. Go with Mr. Montmercy to the public house, give him an accounting of your claims, and trust that you will see your money with interest as promised, for if you do not, we shall be here all night."

The creditors looked at one another in some confusion.

"Get out!" the justice bellowed.

They jumped to obey.

As soon as they had left with Mr. Montmercy, the justice leaned over the table and, taking Aurora's hand, put it to his lips. "You may be seated now, Miss Valentin, and thank you for your assistance to this court, er, convocation."

Ryder watched her take up the paper, fold it neatly and replace it in her sleeve. Sedately, she moved to her seat. She looked everywhere but at him. He began to be impatient for an end to the proceedings so that he might go to her, take her face in his hands and compel her to look at him.

"Mr. Starr," said Justice Conkle, interrupting Ryder's thoughts, "we have now before us a charge of theft against you. Please do not take it amiss. I am sure no offence is meant."

"No offence is taken, I assure you."

"Excellent. Now, did you or did you not embezzle two thousand pounds from the diocese?"

What remained of the gallery exploded at the mention of the sum. Vainly, the justice shouted for silence.

When Mr. Starr rose again, the room quieted. "I believe there is a slight error," he said. "The sum in question is two pounds sixpence."

At this, the justice sat back and rubbed his tired eyes. "Mr. Starr, if you are so beneficent as to repay those snivelling fellows and their damned lawyers, may I assume that you will have no objection to repaying two pounds sixpence?"

"You may. As soon as I am able, I shall repay it with interest."

The bishop stood and, wiping a tear from the corner of his eye, exclaimed, "Oh, Ryder, I shall pay you your quarter's wages so that you may pay it at once and not have to wait for the codicil to be proved, but I should be honoured if you would allow me to pay the sum myself."

"No, no, Bishop. I insist upon paying."

"Oh, but it was I who wronged you."

"It was I who wronged you, sir."

Justice Conkle interrupted, saying ill naturedly, "Bishop, may we dispense with these disgusting displays of sentiment? As Mr. Starr is our guest in Sudsbury, we owe him the hospitality of granting his wishes. You will give him his wages and permit him to repay the sum this very day, and that, I hope, is the last word on the subject."

Nodding agreement, the bishop sat.

"There is yet another charge against the prisoner: to wit, that he did wilfully and knowingly escape from the Sudsbury jail, overcoming Mr. Gunion, the jailer, with superior strength and a pistol smuggled to him by a person or persons unknown, that he rode as far as Worcestershire, where he was apprehended by said Mr. Gunion and returned to the place of his incarceration forthwith."

Mr. Gunion rose and cried, "You will not hang a man for availing himself of a bit of a gallop, will you? He meant no harm, I take my oath, and he came back willingly."

"No, I shall not hang him, Mr. Gunion. In fact, I have a mind to dismiss the matter entirely, for if Mr. Starr is innocent of the other charges, then he ought not to have been in jail in the first place, and so his riding off to the next county may be construed as a brief holiday, and a well-deserved one, too, I might add."

"Thank you, Justice," Ryder said.

"Not at all. It's the least I can do, given that you permitted me to beat you at cards every night this week." He rose, slammed a book on the table and roared, "I declare this court, er, this convocation, adjourned!"

"You cannot adjourn!" a voice cried from the gallery. Farmer Guggins, who had not joined the others at the tavern, now moved to the justice's table. "There is another charge agin the man."

"I am aware of no other charges," said the justice, adjusting his wig over his ears. "Do you know of any, Mr. Starr?"

Ryder confessed that he knew of none. However, based on his past adventures, it did not surprise him to learn that he might be called on to pay the piper yet again.

"He's been guilty of a breach of promise," stated the farmer, "and I mean to have satisfaction on my daughter's behalf!"

The ladies and gentlemen in the gallery stirred with excitement. As entertaining as the proceedings had proved thus far, they promised to wax even juicier now. Nothing was so conducive to amusement as the discovery of seduction.

Farmer Guggins stepped forward to say, "I have brought my daughter, Justice, whom Lord Matchless there must be made to marry."

Ryder would have smiled at this absurd turn of events had he not seen Aurora grow pale. Her gravity deepened, and he guessed her thoughts. She had been right about him from the first, she was surely thinking; he was a scoundrel and a liar. Any good opinion she had had of him must now be dashed. At this moment, he would have forfeited any chance to inherit a title and wealth to have been able to say he was not the rogue she thought him.

"I beg your pardon, Mr. Starr," the justice said, "it appears there is yet another charge against you. I hope this does not incommode you."

"Not at all," Ryder replied graciously.

Farmer Guggins now beckoned to his daughter, who, after a shy giggle, stepped forward, tossing her pretty curls and smiling coquettishly at his lordship.

"Now, my young miss," Justice Conkle said, "what have you to say for yourself?"

She half turned, so that she might glance under her lashes at Mr. Starr as she related her tale. "La, sir, Ryder and I love each other with all our hearts and have done since long before he was become an heir to a fortune. Naturally, I never said boo about it to my father on account of Ryder's being so poor and Papa's hating him so much that he fell into a snit at the mention of his name. Nor did I press poor Ryder on account of his Fontinella, who was his lady-love that broke his heart when she died. But as Ryder is no longer poor and as it has come to light that there was no Fontinella, that she was purely a little joke of Ryder's, nothing need stand in our way, and so I thought we should be married."

A black cloud descended on Justice Conkle's brow. "Did he induce you to submit to him with promises of marriage?"

She patted her curls and turned the full force of her large blue eyes on the justice. "I do not remember."

Mr. Starr stood. "May I interject here, Justice, that I knew the young lady to be pious and virtuous in the extreme. I therefore did not presume to ask her to submit to my wicked will, and though she is everything that is charming and beautiful, I never promised marriage to her. Furthermore, I have a witness who will so swear. Mr. Nussle."

"Is that true, Mr. Nussle?"

Nussle stood and, as was his habit, corroborated the claim in a lofty tone. "I can state unequivocally, and would be willing to swear to it on any number of Testaments, that Master Ryder never offered marriage. It was always the ladies who offered marriage to him."

With swiftly waning patience, the justice said, "Miss Guggins, his lordship contends that there was neither seduction nor an offer of marriage. Where there is no such circumstance, there is no breach of promise, and where there is no breach of promise, there is no reason for this court, that is to say, this convocation, to continue another moment. And so I invite you to go away and find something useful to do with yourself."

"Oh, but Justice," the young lady cried, "though he did not offer marriage then, there is no reason why he cannot do so now, is there?"

Justice Conkle frowned. "Mr. Starr, the young lady wishes to know whether you might possibly offer marriage now. Would you be so good as to give her an answer so that we may all go home and have our dinner?"

Ryder said without hesitation, "I cannot offer for her now."

"Oh, but why not?" she pouted.

"There is a perfectly good reason, my dear Miss Guggins."

"La, to be sure there is, my sweet. What is it?"

"You ask what it is? Well, I shall tell you. I shall tell you this instant. Nussle, tell the young lady why I cannot offer for her at this time."

Rising again, Nussle straightened his shoulders. "Certainly, sir." He fixed Miss Guggins and the horde of onlookers with his iciest glare of condescension. "The reason that Master Ryder cannot offer marriage to you is that he is already betrothed, to that young lady there."

Following the direction of his finger, all eyes fell on Aurora, who appeared to sense that she was the focus of a hundred and twenty stares. She looked up from her hands and gazed round the room. Ryder watched her complexion go from white to pink to bright crimson.

He shook his head and despaired. Nussle had miscalculated this time. If there was one thing Miss Aurora Valentin would not do—was incapable of doing—it was telling a boldfaced lie. Even if she loved him to the depths of her soul, she would be incapable of lying for him. Even to save his undeserving neck from the gallows or, what was worse, from the yoke of matrimony, she would not, could not do it.

"Miss Valentin," said the justice, "is this true? Are you indeed betrothed to Mr. Starr?"

Slowly, Aurora rose and swallowed hard. As he watched her, Ryder sought desperately for a way to spare her. The only notion that came to mind was striding to her side, lifting her into his arms, and carrying her off. But before he could execute this dashing plan, she said, in a voice that reminded him achingly of a melody, "Justice Conkle, I love Mr. Starr. It is not surprising, therefore, that I should like nothing better than to marry him and live with him the rest of my life."

AURORA NOTED with pleasure that the effect of this declaration was profound. As noisy as the hall had been earlier, it was now twenty times as quiet. The townsfolk regarded her with prodigious interest. The ladies of the book society simpered and poked each other with their elbows, as if to say they had known what was afoot all along. Miss Guggins levelled a glare at her, accompanied by a protruding lower lip. Farmer Guggins stalked from the vestibule, muttering under his breath. The justice patted his wig and endeavoured to stifle a yawn. Nussle gave her a smile of unmistakable triumph. And her father wiped teardrops from his cheek, whispering that he was the happiest of men.

She did not dare look at Ryder. It had been impossible to look at him for the entire day. If he had returned her glance with teasing, she would have dissolved. If he had returned it with anger, she would have wilted. If he had returned it with affection, she would have melted. Any way one looked at it, she would have been done for. Therefore, she fixed her eyes on the floor and said politely to Justice Conkle, "May I have a word in private with Mr. Starr?"

"Indeed you may!" pronounced the justice, jumping up. "I declare this convocation closed." He slammed his hand on the table. "Everybody is to go away now and not come back until the next assize. Shoo, all of you."

With such barkings did he drive the crowd from the hall. As the last one to leave, he bade farewell to Mr. Starr, saying, "I hope this matter has been concluded to your satisfaction, sir. I am very sorry you were subjected to such proceedings, but it could not be helped, and I hope you will recall us kindly if you should indeed be elevated to the earldom. In any case, all's well that ends well, and do not forget that you owe me three shillings for beating you at whist."

When he had gone, Aurora turned to Ryder. Slowly, she approached him and, for the first time, ventured to meet his eyes. His intense look daunted her, but she did not falter. After all, she told herself, she had done nothing but speak the truth. If he still doubted her, she must convince him otherwise. She would not, of course, dream of interfering, but she would move Heaven and Earth to persuade him that she loved him in earnest.

As she drew close, she removed the paper from her sleeve and handed it to him.

He glanced at her face, then the paper, then her face again.

"Please, read it," she said.

Tearing his eyes from her, he read. Finished, he looked up.

"I came upon it in the library at Broome Court. Your cousin had hidden it. He meant to destroy it, but died before he had the opportunity. Ryder, you must know what it means. Your uncle did value you."

She saw that he was moved, though nobody else living would have thought so.

With difficulty, he said, "I ought to have trusted him. It is difficult for a rogue to trust, however. He judges everybody by his own conduct."

"You had every right to doubt me, for though I had no intention of trapping you, I did go to your bedchamber to find out what I could about your commerce with Mr. Aycock. I had no notion you would come in, and certainly none that you would be glad to see me. I am so sorry, Ryder."

"Why did you refuse to look at me today?"

"If I had looked at you, I should have been compelled to kiss you."

"Oh."

"Say you are no longer angry with me."

Passionately, he said, "Of course I am angry. You ought never to have gone to see my cousin. I was obliged to come after you and see to your safety, as you were unwilling to see to it yourself. Heaven knows what might have happened to you. I might have lost you altogether."

She smiled. "Thank you for coming. As you saw, I was perfectly well. But you will think me heartless, Ryder. When your poor cousin died, all I could think of was that your last hope might be gone. It was a ridiculous notion, for I had the codicil in my hand, or rather, in my sleeve, but I was too distressed to think clearly. It was some time before I gave any thought to his lordship. I cannot imagine what caused me to be so unfeeling."

"Perhaps it was what you told the justice and the entire town—that you love me."

She nodded. "Perhaps."

A glow of mischief lit his eyes. "That was a most charitable thing to say, Miss Valentin."

"Charitable!" Her eyes flashed. "How dare you ascribe my words to charity! How can you so misconstrue my motives? You knew I disliked you because I liked you. How can you not know that I love you because I love you?"

His hand reached behind her and he drew her to him. "I do know. I just wanted to hear you say it again, when nobody else was listening."

She sighed as he stroked her hair. "Dear Ryder, you are a wicked, wicked man."

"Allow me to demonstrate just how wicked." He kissed her with a sweetness that belied his profession of wickedness. It was as if he wished to mark every second of their intimacy with a touch, each one lighter than the last. "I hope you will not object," he said, "to my standing so close."

By way of reply, she planted an unhurried kiss on his lips. That called forth a different response, one that inspired her, as soon as she could take a breath, to scan the hall to see if anybody had stayed to observe.

He enclosed her totally in his arms. "There is only one thing wanting to make our happiness complete. Marry me."

She pushed away. Sadly, she shook her head.

Protesting, he said, "But not minutes ago, you declared that you wished to marry me. There were at least sixty witnesses."

"Yes, I did say that, and I meant it."

"I have never before asked a lady to marry me, though a good many of them wished I had."

"I have no doubt of it."

"Well, then, I ought to be rewarded for my wonderful reformation."

"It is impossible. I cannot leave my father. It will be hard enough that he must lose his secretary. He will be entirely lost if I leave him as well."

"Ah, I see. It is your father, and not my character or conduct, which keeps you from becoming Mrs. Starr—or possibly Lady Matchless."

"Why should your character or conduct prevent me?"

"Because, my love, I am a rogue."

She smiled. "I know. You are also adorable."

This produced a groan. "Aurora, I shall be ousted from the fraternity if it gets out that I am adorable." Pulling her to him, he vowed, "I have no recourse but to to find a way to keep you forever silent on the subject."

EPILOGUE

AFTER A SCOURING of the peerage, parish records and wills stretching back for generations, Mr. Starr was found to be the closest living relation of the deceased Matchlesses and was thus declared to be the next Earl. Upon his elevation, he immediately set about restoring Broome Court and repaying the gentlemen who had been kind enough to finance his adventures over the past year. That done, he was eager to begin the work of providing himself with a family, and a large one at that.

Ryder and Aurora fretted for some weeks over the means of informing the bishop of their wish to marry. Each time they were on the point of doing so, they held back, unwilling to desolate the poor man. Meanwhile, they conducted a courtship that they flattered themselves was secret.

One morning, Ryder rode from Broome Court in time to take breakfast with Aurora. Afterwards, they adjourned to the lawn and sought out the fountain among the hedges. There they twined their arms about each other, and while he kissed her under the shade of the elms, she sighed and pretended to be enchanted with his loverlike twaddle.

"I shall never draw an easy breath until I make you mine," he declared.

"I am overcome, sir, and shall be thine at thy earliest convenience."

He grew serious. "I wish that were true."

Taking his hand, she said softly, "We will not despair, Ryder. We will speak to my father. Very soon."

"It is poetic justice, I expect, that now, when I am finally in a hurry to be married, I should be plagued with obstacles."

"Here is your poetic justice." Standing on tiptoe, she chastely kissed his brow.

That being not at all what suited him, he kissed her unchastely on the mouth.

Thus they were discovered by the bishop, who, observing their billing and cooing, asked, "When are you to be married? I hope you will not delay it long."

They looked at each other.

"I thought you would not like it, Papa."

The bishop cried, "Oh, it is what I should like above anything!"

"You would not object to my taking Aurora from Sudsbury?" his lordship asked.

"No, for I intend to go with her."

"But, Papa, as bishop you must live in the cathedral town."

"I do not intend to be bishop any longer."

The earl replied, "Aurora and I cannot allow you to give up the bishopric for our sake."

"It is no sacrifice, dear boy. The one who ought to have been bishop was Mrs. Valentin. I never liked it, you know. And now that my daughter is to be married and I may go and live with her, I need not continue any longer to do what I dislike. Of course, your mother will not approve, Aurora. But I shall have to take up the matter with her in the next life. As for this one, I shall do as I please in it."

"But what will you do, Papa? After so many years of devotion to the Church, you cannot be idle."

"I do not intend to be idle. I shall write novels in the Gothic style, like Monk Lewis. I shall invent tales of evil princes, dark castles, secret passageways, deranged prisoners in the attic, murders and tortures and such."

Again, Aurora and Ryder exchanged glances.

"Papa, you are the gentlest man in the world. You cannot be capable of writing such horror."

The bishop grinned shyly. "I never told your mother, for it would have made her as cross as crabs, but I find it vastly pleasant to be bloodthirsty from time to time."

Laughing, Ryder said, "Well, Bishop, you shall be bloodthirsty to your heart's content." Turning to Aurora, he invited, "And you, Miss Valentin, will be my bride, unless you can think of another objection."

As she could think of none, the promise was sealed. The bishop went on his way to plot his first novel, while the young people plotted their future, which, they determined, was to be filled with as much merriment as any two people in love could cram into a lifetime.

**Relive the romance...
Harlequin and Silhouette
are proud to present**

by Request

A program of collections of three complete novels by the most
requested authors with the most requested themes. Be sure to
look for one volume each month with three complete novels by
top name authors.

In June: **NINE MONTHS** Penny Jordan
                             Stella Cameron
                             Janice Kaiser

**Three women pregnant and alone. But a lot can
happen in nine months!**

In July: **DADDY'S**   Kristin James
            HOME   Naomi Horton
                            Mary Lynn Baxter

**Daddy's Home... and his presence is long
overdue!**

In August: **FORGOTTEN**   Barbara Kaye
            PAST   Pamela Browning
                            Nancy Martin

**Do you dare to create a future if you've forgotten
the past?**

Available at your favorite retail outlet.

HARLEQUIN®   Silhouette

REQ-G

Fifty red-blooded, white-hot, true-blue hunks from every State in the Union!

Beginning in May, look for MEN MADE IN AMERICA! Written by some of our most popular authors, these stories feature fifty of the strongest, sexiest men, each from a different state in the union!

Two titles available every other month at your favorite retail outlet.

In September, look for:

DECEPTIONS by Annette Broadrick (California)
STORMWALKER by Dallas Schulze (Colorado)

In November, look for:

STRAIGHT FROM THE HEART by Barbara Delinsky (Connecticut)
AUTHOR'S CHOICE by Elizabeth August (Delaware)

You won't be able to resist MEN MADE IN AMERICA!

good

Calloway Corners

In September, Harlequin is proud to bring readers four involving, romantic stories about the Calloway sisters, set in Calloway Corners, Louisiana. Written by four of Harlequin's most popular and award-winning authors, you'll be enchanted by these sisters and the men they love!

MARIAH by Sandra Canfield
JO by Tracy Hughes
TESS by Katherine Burton
EDEN by Penny Richards

As an added bonus, you can enter a sweepstakes contest to win a trip to Calloway Corners, and meet all four authors. Watch for details in all Calloway Corners books in September.